GIFTED

Finders Keepers

D1142988

Marilyn Kaye is a bestselling American author. Her Replica series was an international success. Her other series include Camp Sunnyside Friends, After School Club, Out of This World and Last on Earth. She lives in Paris.

Also available:

Gifted: Out of Sight, Out of Mind

Gifted: Better Late Than Never

Gifted: Here Today, Gone Tomorrow

GIFTED

FINDERS
KEEPERS

MARILYN KAYE

MACMILLAN CHILDREN'S BOOKS

First published 2010 by Macmillan Children's Books
a division of Macmillan Publishers Limited
20 New Wharf Road, London N1 9RR
Basingstoke and Oxford
Associated companies throughout the world
www.panmacmillan.com

ISBN 978-0-330-51005-9

3 5 7 9 8 6 4 2

A CIP catalogue record for this book is available from
the British Library.

Typeset by Ellipsis Books Limited, Glasgow
Printed and bound in the UK by CPI Mackays, Chatham ME5 8TD

*For my god-daughter, Rose, her brother, Marius,
and their parents, Isabelle Benech and Laurent Loiseau,
with love*

CHAPTER ONE

KEN WAS TRYING TO ignore the voice in his head.

Everyone else in the room was involved in a lively debate with Madame, their teacher. His classmates were paying attention, and they actually looked interested. Even Jenna Kelley, who generally affected an expression of boredom, was getting into it.

'What's the big deal, Madame? OK, so maybe there are bad guys out there who want to get their hands on us. But we can take care of ourselves. We're gifted, for crying out loud!'

'Yes, you have gifts,' Madame responded patiently, 'but you don't know how to use them properly.'

Sarah spoke softly. 'Wouldn't it be better if we just didn't use them at all?'

'And let the bad guys use them?' Charles asked. 'No way. We have to fight back!'

'Couldn't we just stay away from the bad guys?' Emily wanted to know.

'That's easier said than done,' Tracey pointed out. 'I'm with Charles. We have to be prepared to do battle.'

Madame was getting frustrated. 'But you can't go to battle when you don't know how to use your weapons!'

Ken wanted to be a part of this argument – to listen and maybe even join in. But how could he participate when some old dead guy was yelling at him?

Listen, kid, ya gotta help me! Talk to my grand-daughter – make her see some sense. If she marries that no-good scoundrel, she'll regret it for the rest of her life!

Nobody else could hear the man – only Ken. This was his so-called gift. And he hated it.

This voice was louder than most of the voices he heard. Ken thought maybe the man was hard of hearing. His own grandfather couldn't hear very well and he talked really loud. Ken had to yell back at him to be heard.

At least with *this* old guy Ken wouldn't have to yell. He only had to think his response and the man would hear him. Ken didn't understand how this wordless communication worked. It was just the way it happened.

He 'spoke' to the man. *Look, I'm sorry, but I can't help you out. I don't even know your granddaughter.*

The man replied, *I'll give you her address.*

Ken wondered if the man could hear his silent groan. He didn't know what else to tell him. With other voices he could be tough, even rude, ordering them to leave him alone and get out of his head. But how could he be nasty and disrespectful to an old man?

'Ken? Ken!'

This voice was coming from outside his head. Madame spoke sharply, and to Ken's relief her stern tone drove the dead grandfather away.

'Are you listening, Ken? We're talking about something important.'

'I'm *trying* to listen,' he replied.

Her stern expression softened slightly. 'Is someone bothering you?'

'He's gone now,' Ken told her.

'Good. Then pay attention, because this concerns all of you. Surely by now you've all realized that there are forces in this world who present a grave threat to you. Be aware. Be alert. And never, never let anyone know what you're capable of doing.'

From the corner of his eye, Ken saw Amanda yawn. She politely covered her mouth with her hand, but she was directly in Madame's line of vision and the teacher saw her.

'Am I boring you, Amanda?' she asked, making no effort to hide the annoyance in her tone.

'No, Madame. I just have something else on my mind. Something I need to tell the class.'

'And I'm sure it's something very important,' Madame said smoothly. 'You'll be able share it with us later. Right now, I need your full attention. It's very important that you all realize how your gifts could be exploited. I don't want to frighten you, but you need to be aware of the danger. Do you understand this?'

Jenna raised her hand. 'Amanda thinks you're exaggerating, Madame.'

Madame frowned. 'Jenna, I've told you again and again, you are *not* to read minds in this class.' Her eyes shifted to Amanda. 'And I am *not* exaggerating. Perhaps some of you need to recall some recent events. Emily? Emily!'

Ken knew Emily couldn't use hearing voices as an excuse for not paying attention. She was just day-dreaming. Not like an ordinary daydreamer might though. Emily's dreams had a disturbing tendency to come true.

'Emily!' Madame barked. 'Would you mind not thinking about the future and joining us in the present?'

Emily jumped. 'Sorry, Madame.'

'Remind the class of the potential dangers they could encounter.'

'Why me?' Emily asked plaintively.

'Because, if I'm not mistaken, you were the first to encounter a real threat this year.'

Madame was rarely mistaken, and Emily knew this. Still, she looked confused. From behind her, Jenna poked her shoulder.

'Serena Hancock, Em. Does the name ring a bell?'

Emily slumped back in her seat. 'Oh, right. The student teacher.'

'Would you remind the class what Serena did to you?' Madame asked.

Emily was clearly uncomfortable, but she obeyed. 'She hypnotized me and tried to make me tell her the winning lottery numbers for the next draw.'

'And why did Serena choose you as her victim?' Madame prompted her. 'Why didn't she threaten Jenna, for example, or Sarah?'

Emily sighed. 'Because she knew I could see into the future.'

'Precisely,' Madame declared. 'She knew what you could do, and she wanted to exploit this. Let's move on to another example of a recent threat.' She looked pointedly at Jenna.

The goth-girl scowled.

Madame spoke briskly. 'I know it's a painful memory, Jenna, but it's important that we remember.'

Jenna gave an elaborate shrug. 'It wasn't *painful*, just boring.'

Ken caught Amanda's eye, and they exchanged

knowing looks. This was so Jenna – to act tough, like nothing could really upset her. Not even a man showing up out of nowhere and claiming to be the father who had disappeared before Jenna was even born. Not even when this man turned out to be a fraud, someone who wanted to use Jenna's mind-reading skills to win a lot of money at poker.

'Wait a second,' Charles broke in. 'What happened to Emily and what happened to Jenna just happened to *them*. This doesn't have anything to do with the rest of us.'

'I disagree,' Madame said. 'What threatens one of us threatens all of us. I cannot stress this enough. We need to think of ourselves as a team.'

Ken hoped his own reaction to that notion didn't show in his expression. He respected Madame and all that, but to call this class a team – that was completely bogus. Ken knew all about teams – as an athlete he'd played on lots of them, including Meadowbrook's soccer team. And he'd been on teams in other classes – working on science projects, stuff like that. Being on a team meant being connected in some way, working together towards a common goal. Looking around this room, he couldn't imagine working with any of his classmates. And he certainly didn't feel connected to any of them. Even without the gifts, they had nothing in common. Jenna was a sullen goth-girl with a less-than-stellar reputation. Amanda was a super-popular queen bee. Even though he wasn't involved in playing football any more, Ken still considered himself a jock. There was no one else in the class who was even interested in sport.

And each of them dealt with their gifts in different ways. Space cadet Emily sometimes acted like her gift frightened her. Amanda wasn't too crazy about her gift, and Sarah absolutely refused to use hers. Only whiney, wimpy Martin and Charles who was stuck in a wheelchair seemed like they enjoyed the powers their gifts gave them. And what about Carter? Who could have anything in common with a total mystery? The strange, silent boy was little more than a zombie.

As far as Ken was concerned, the only thing they all shared was this class. The gifts – and the students who had them – didn't have any connection at all.

Sometimes, like now, he wondered if Madame had a gift like Jenna's. At that very moment she was looking at him, and she could have been reading his mind.

'I realize that you might not think of yourselves as a team, but that may well be how our enemies think of us. Surely I don't need to remind you of your most recent adventure?' When there was no response to that, she shook her head wearily. 'Or maybe I do. Amanda, would you please refresh our memory?'

Martin piped up. 'Why are you asking *her*? She wasn't even there!'

'Yes, I was!' Amanda snapped.

Martin glared at her. 'Hey, I'm not stupid. I would have noticed if you were there. It was me, Tracey, Emily and Sarah. Oh, and Carter was there for a while at the beginning.'

Sarah spoke gently. 'I wasn't really there, Martin. Amanda had taken over my body. I didn't get there till the very end.'

'I can't believe you didn't know that, Martin,' Tracey declared. 'Didn't you notice Sarah wasn't acting like herself?'

Jenna snorted. 'Are you kidding? Martin never pays attention to anyone but himself.'

Charles laughed. 'I'll bet Martin was too scared to notice anything.'

'I wasn't scared,' Martin replied hotly.

'You sure acted like you were,' Tracey said.

'*Tracey!*' Madame said in a warning tone, and the other students frowned at Tracey too. Teasing Martin was a big no-no. That was when his 'gift' came out, and nobody was eager to see mass destruction or suffer personal bodily injury, which might easily happen if Martin's super-strength kicked in. Of course, Tracey wouldn't have to worry if Martin went on one of his rampages. She could always disappear. Personally, Ken thought she had the most interesting gift of all of them.

'Let's get back to the subject,' Madame said. 'Amanda, could you give us a brief synopsis of what happened to some of you?'

'We were kidnapped,' she said, 'by this woman named Clare and two men.'

Tracey supplied the names. 'Howard and George.'

'Yeah, whatever,' Amanda said dismissively. 'They were just flunkies. Clare was in charge. Anyway, they wanted us to rob banks for them. They took Carter first, then Tracey, Martin and Sarah. And Emily.'

Madame nodded. 'And they chose each of you for a reason. Emily could predict the scene at the bank, Martin could break down doors, Tracey could sneak into the vault without being seen. And Sarah could force people to do whatever the robbers needed them to do.'

'Except they didn't really have Sarah,' Emily noted. 'They got Amanda instead.'

Jenna laughed. 'I almost feel sorry for the bad guys. Can you imagine getting stuck with Amanda? It's not like she could help anyone rob a bank.' She paused. 'Actually, I take that back. Maybe she would have helped with the robbery if she thought the vault contained shoes. Or handbags. Otherwise her gift is pretty worthless.'

Amanda's obsession with fashion was well known, and everyone laughed – except Carter, of course, who never smiled or laughed or showed any emotion at all on his face. Which made Ken think about something that had puzzled him ever since the kid-nappings.

'Why did they want Carter?' he asked out loud.

The room fell silent, and everyone turned to look at the figure sitting right at the back. As usual, the pale, round-faced boy wasn't perturbed by the sudden attention. His expression was as blank as it always was. Ken knew everyone had to be thinking the same thing: did Carter even have a gift? Or was he only in this class because he was – well – weird?

Charles broke the silence. 'I want to know why they didn't kidnap *me*. I've got *real* power.'

Charles was known for his bragging, but no one could deny the truth in what he was saying. Being able to make things move with his mind could have made him very useful to someone with criminal intents.

Emily had an answer for him. 'The house didn't have disabled access, Charles. The doorways were too narrow for a wheelchair and you wouldn't have been able to get up the stairs.'

'Clearly the kidnappers had done their home-work,' Madame said. 'They knew who they wanted, who they could use. This is what I want to impress upon you. There are people out there who know all about you. And if those people ever got together and pooled their information . . .'

Sarah spoke. 'You're saying we're all at risk.'

'Exactly,' Madame replied.

'Except Ken,' Charles piped up.

Madame frowned. 'Why do you say that, Charles?'

'Dead people talk to him – big deal! How is that going to help a criminal?'

Martin joined in. 'Yeah, his gift is totally useless.'

'You don't know that,' Madame declared. 'I'm sure there are people who would find Ken's gift extremely interesting.' She looked at Ken, as if she wanted him to back her up.

Ken just shrugged. Because in all honesty, he pretty much agreed with both Martin and Charles on this subject.

Madame continued. 'Now, I'd like you all to share your thoughts on how you can best protect yourselves from exploitation.'

Several hands went up, but Ken's wasn't one of

them. As far as he was concerned, he'd rather learn how to protect himself from his own gift.

From the very beginning, when he realized he had this gift, it had been nothing but a headache. At first he thought he could use it to help a certain dead person with a problem left unresolved on earth, and he had tried – he'd really tried – to respond to this person's needs. But the result had been disastrous, and now he, Ken, had an ongoing problem to deal with. He hadn't been bothered by it much lately, but there was no telling when that problem would pop up again. Just thinking about the possibility gave him a headache, and he pushed it out of his head.

OK, maybe there had been a couple of times when his gift had been useful. He'd been able to alert Jenna to the fact that the man who claimed to be her father was a fraud after Ken got a message from beyond the grave that confirmed it. And he'd learned the whereabouts of a guy who'd helped kidnap some of Ken's classmates when the kidnapper's late mother told Ken where to find her son.

But events like that were rare. Most of the time the voices made demands. And ever since that first demand, the one that turned into a mess, he'd made every effort to ignore them. It wasn't easy. There were so many dead people, so many sad stories. Many of them wanted him to communicate a message to someone left behind. A man might ask him to apologize to a friend for something he'd done when he was alive. A woman would ask him to tell her husband that she'd loved him. A thief who'd repented might want him to return money he'd stolen, and other people asked Ken to deliver souvenirs. One time, there had been a man who wanted him to tell the police that his death wasn't an accident – that his ex-wife had killed him.

But Ken didn't want to get involved. He'd done that once, and he was still paying the price. Besides, how could he do what they asked?

Excuse me, Miss, but your dead grandfather thinks your boyfriend is no good.

Excuse me, Officer, but do you remember the man who died when he fell down the stairs? And you thought it was an accident? Well, I know for a fact that his wife pushed him.

They wouldn't believe him. How could he

possibly explain what he knew without telling them how he got the information? And then they'd think he was nuts. Besides, as Madame was constantly telling them, they should never let anyone know about their gifts.

So if Ken couldn't do anything with his gift, his only option was to get rid of it, to make every effort to silence the voices. And he'd been getting a little better at it. Pleading, arguing, ordering the spirits to go away and leave him alone was beginning to have an effect. He had to be tough with them, get angry – even nasty sometimes. He hated being rude, but what else could he do?

Ken . . . Hey, Ken, what's up, man? Are you there? Can you listen?

Ken slumped back in his seat. This was the one voice he could never order to leave him alone.

Yeah, I'm listening.

And as the voice in his head began to talk, Ken's thoughts went back to how it all began for him . . .

CHAPTER TWO

SOME PEOPLE HATED THE first day back at school after a vacation. Not Ken Preston. Why would he be unhappy about it or unwilling to return to the place where he ruled?

Of course, he wasn't the only king at Meadowbrook. There were plenty of other popular guys. But in all modesty, he had to admit that he was way up there, on the upper rung of the middle-school social ladder.

'Yo, Preston! Hey man, what's up?'

Ken saluted the freckled, red-haired boy who strode towards him. 'Hey, Jack. How was California?'

'Extremely cool,' Jack Farrell told him. 'Not much in the way of surf, but lots of action on the beach, if you know what I mean.' He whistled. 'I'm telling ya, man, those California girls are a completely different kind of female species.'

Ken laughed. In this particular way, Jack had always been a little more mature than the rest of the gang. 'Better not let Lucy hear you say that.'

'I just looked, I didn't touch,' Jack assured him. 'Not like any of them would let me get close enough to do that anyway. Blondes in bikinis are out of my league. What about you? Did you have any adventures with the opposite sex this summer?'

'Not really.' They were inside the building now, and Ken lowered his voice. 'Well, actually, I kissed Amanda Beeson underwater at Sophie Greene's pool party last month.'

'Oh, yeah? You like her?'

'It was a dare,' Ken explained with a shrug. 'I barely know her. And I haven't seen her since.'

'She's pretty hot,' Jack mused.

'Yeah, I guess. Not really my type, though. I think she's kind of a snob.'

They rounded the corner to the hall where lockers lined the wall. A whoop went up from three boys gathered at one of the lockers, and Ken and Jack paused to greet them.

'Guess we'll be seeing you two at practice this afternoon,' one of them said.

Ken grinned. 'Yeah, we thought we might drop by.' He and Jack were captain and vice-captain of Meadowbrook's soccer team that year. 'See ya there.'

They moved on, and Jack stopped at a door. 'Here we are.'

Ken opened a notebook and looked at the print-out of his class schedule. 'Not me. I've got homeroom in one-one-eight.'

Jack gave a look of exaggerated dismay. 'You're kidding! They're splitting us up?'

Ken shrugged. 'Guess so. We had a good run though. Two years in the same homeroom. What else have you got on the schedule?'

The boys compared timetables and discovered they had their lunch breaks and English classes together.

'Excellent,' Jack proclaimed. 'I'll eat your lunch and you'll write my essays.'

'Dream on, pal,' Ken responded. 'Later.' He moved on down the hall to his own homeroom.

At least a dozen students were already seated in

the classroom when he entered. A pretty blonde girl perked up when she saw him.

'Ken, hi!' She indicated the chair next to hers. 'Nobody's sitting here.'

Ken couldn't remember her name, but he gave her a friendly smile anyway. He'd been getting a lot of attention like this from girls lately. 'Thanks, but I like the back of the room. Less chance of getting called on.' He joined the four boys who already lined the wall at the far end.

He was greeted with welcoming smiles and the usual calls of 'Hey, man!'

Ken slapped hands as he moved to the end of the row. He knew them all. None of them were on the soccer team, but Ken had never limited his socializing to the jocks. Funny thing though – when people knew you were an athlete, they thought your only interest was sports.

'You gonna get that lousy team of ours out of the dumps?' one boy asked with a grin.

'Absolutely,' Ken assured him. 'We're going all the way to the finals this year. Farrell and I have big plans!'

The warning bell sounded and a wave of students rushed into the room, followed by a teacher. Then the final bell rang and the teacher spoke.

'Hello. My name is Mr Kingston, and—'

That was as far as he got before the intercom on the wall emitted a shrill buzz, indicating that the High and Mighty was about to address them.

First came the voice of the secretary. 'May I have your attention for the morning announcements?'

In keeping with tradition, the students in the class yelled out, '*No!*' Naturally, this had no effect.

The next voice was booming and authoritative. 'Good morning, students, this is your principal. I'd like to take this opportunity to welcome you back to Meadowbrook Middle School.'

Since this was the third time Ken had heard Mr Jackson's first-day-of-school speech, he knew what was coming – the usual exhortations to do well, study hard, behave properly, blah, blah, blah. He tuned out the principal and thought about his own plans for the new school term.

This year, ninth grade, would be his last year at Meadowbrook, and he needed to leave his mark on the middle school. He'd already had two good years here and he wanted this one to be outstanding. Next September he'd be a lowly underclassman at Central High School, so he was determined to enjoy this final year of being on top of the heap.

First of all he'd lead the soccer team to the play-offs, maybe even to the state championship. This would take some real work. He was relying on his popularity with his teammates to keep them enthused and practising harder and longer than they had the year before. If they had a good season, his reputation could secure him a place on Central's varsity team. Most high school freshmen were stuck playing on Central's B team, but Ken knew they made exceptions for exceptional players. And if he became a star on Central's team, a scout might notice him and he could be up for a university scholarship.

But Ken was a realist. He knew there had to be lots of soccer players as good as he was, and he knew he couldn't count on soccer to provide him with a university education. He had to keep his marks up too. What he'd said to that blonde-haired girl about sitting in the back of a classroom so he wouldn't be called on wasn't really true. He'd always done pretty well at school, and he was proud of it. If he did really well this year he could get advanced placement classes at Central, which would give his parents a big thrill.

As for his social life, he had some goals in that area too. Most of his classmates didn't really go out on 'dates' – they just hung out in groups. But lately his friends had started pairing off. Jack and Lucy had been together since last spring. Ken was beginning to think it might be kind of fun to know one girl really well, to talk to her on the phone every night, exchange text messages on their cell phones and meet between classes. Not to mention what they might get up to when they were alone. Ken grinned to himself. Yes, there were definite advantages to having a girlfriend.

But what girl? Amanda Beeson? Jack was right – she was pretty hot. He didn't much like the clique she hung out with though. It seemed to consist of a lot of girls who were mean to other girls. And Amanda was rumoured to be one of the meanest. He remembered the previous year when she'd been in one of his classes, and she'd said some really nasty things to that strange, sad girl, Tracey . . . Something. It was weird, but Ken couldn't begin to recall her last name.

Anyway, there were plenty of other girls. And even though Ken would never admit it publicly, he knew many of them wouldn't mind hanging out with him. Like that blonde in the front of his homeroom. What was *her* name? Ken shook his head ruefully. Not such a great start to finding a girlfriend. But someone would turn up in the end.

His first day back at school progressed nicely. Some of the teachers were halfway decent. In his Civics class they were going to debate capital punishment, they would dissect crayfish in Biology, and in English they were going to read modern novels, so there wouldn't be any of that 'thee' and 'thou' stuff he hated.

But what he really looked forward to would come after all the classes – his first day as captain of Meadowbrook's soccer team.

After changing into his football kit, he met with Jack and Coach Holloway in the coach's office for a private consultation. As usual, Coach Holloway looked worried.

'You guys have a lot of work to do. We don't have a decent goalie and the whole team looks flabby. I don't know how we're going to whip them into shape for the season.'

Jack responded in his typically cocky way. 'No sweat, Coach. Leave them to us. We can handle them.'

Ken was a little less optimistic, especially after they met up with the whole team on the field. A lazy summer filled with too many picnics had taken its toll, and they all looked pretty pathetic.

'You do the pep talk,' Jack whispered to Ken.

'Why me?'

'Because people like you better.'

Ken grinned. This was true – Jack could be a show-off, and it had been known to get on people's nerves sometimes. Ken didn't particularly like public speaking but he did what he had to do.

'OK, guys, we've got less than one week to pre-pare for our first game. We'll be going up against Sunnydale Middle School. Sunnydale made it to the semi-finals last year, and I'm sure they think they're going to blow us away. It's going to be a battle, but we can be ready for them. We gotta hit 'em hard and show them there have been some big changes here at Meadowbrook.' After a few more encouraging words, he turned the team over to the coach.

'Start off with some laps,' Coach barked. 'Three times around the field.'

This took the wind out of a few boys, but Ken was pleased to see a decent survival rate. After that, Coach put them through a series of gruelling exercises, and finally it was time to practise some real set pieces. The boys split up into two teams, with Ken in charge of one side and Jack taking over the other.

Ken worked on psyching himself up. It wasn't easy seeing your friends – especially your best pal – as your enemy, but that was the only way to get anything out of these mock matches. Squaring his shoulders, he was ready to get down and dirty.

One of the guys kicked the ball, and it flew past him. He took off after it. Glancing over his shoulder, he saw Jack coming up from behind, so he picked up the pace. Then he saw a couple of defenders just ahead, ready to tackle him. He couldn't let that happen. Quickly he passed to Freddie Ryan, who shot the ball back to Ken as soon as he was clear of the defenders. The pass was high and Ken turned to head the ball to another teammate.

The last thing he remembered seeing was Jack's face. And then − darkness.

Complete and utter nothingness. No sensations, nothing to see, nothing to hear. No pain either. Just − nothing. He was without form, floating in space.

At some point he thought he felt a prick in his arm, sharper than a mosquito bite. Another time he was vaguely aware of lights. And then some indistinct voices. Hands on his body, something cold pressed against his chest.

And finally, pain. It was almost a relief, because that was when he knew he wasn't dead.

'Ken? Ken, can you hear me?'

He opened his eyes and saw his mother's anxious face. What was she doing on the soccer field? He tried to sit up, and she rested a hand lightly on his shoulder.

'Don't move, darling. Stay still. George, ring for the nurse!'

George – that was his father. So he was on the field too. This was all very strange. And why were they calling for a nurse?

Then things began happening quickly. He could hear, he could see . . . he was aware. And he realized he was in a hospital.

Gradually the memory of what had happened started to come back to him. He remembered Jack right behind him, moving fast. Apparently the collision had been pretty bad. They'd both been running at full tilt when they hit each other. Both he and Jack must have been knocked out.

'What time is it?' he asked his mother.

'Almost midnight,' she told him. 'How do you feel?'

He winced. 'Everything hurts.'

A nurse appeared. She looked into his eyes, took his pulse, and then gave him an injection. 'This is for the pain,' she told him. Then she had a whispered conversation with his parents, and left.

Ken was trying to think, and it wasn't easy. His

brain seemed to be operating in slow motion. Training had started at four. It must have been nearly five o'clock by the time they started the match. His mother had just told him it was midnight. Twelve minus five . . . simple subtraction made his head hurt, but he persevered.

'I've been unconscious for seven hours?'

His mother spoke gently. 'It's Friday, Ken. You've been in a coma for four days. You had a concussion, some broken ribs, and you've got some badly torn tendons in your left ankle. But you're going to be OK.'

All he really heard was 'Friday'. 'I've got a game tomorrow . . .' and then the rest of her words sunk in. 'I suppose I won't be playing.'

'No, dear. But you're going to be OK eventually. It will take some time though.'

Was she saying he'd be out for the season? he wondered in dismay. Then he realized he hadn't even asked about the other victim.

'How's Jack? Can he play tomorrow?'

The injection the nurse had given him must have been pretty potent. He had drifted off to sleep before he could get an answer, and he wasn't even sure if he'd actually asked the question out loud. Maybe it was the painkilling medication that made his dreams so vivid.

He was back on the soccer pitch, running after a ball. But every time he got close enough to kick it, the ball moved further away. He kept running, the ball kept moving. From behind, he could hear Jack's voice. *Ken, wait for me! Wait up, Ken!* Or maybe he was yelling, *Wake up, Ken, wake up!*

And he did.

He was alone in the hospital room now. Light poured in from the window. He lifted his head and tried to sit up but it was too painful, and his head sank back down on the pillow.

The door opened, and a young woman in a pink pinafore came in wheeling a tray. 'Good morning!' she said in a bright voice. 'How do you feel?'

'OK. It hurts a little.'

'The nurse is coming around with your medication,' she told him. 'How about some breakfast? Are you hungry?'

'No,' he replied, but she didn't pay any attention

to his response. She pressed a button on the bed, and it raised him painlessly into a halfway sitting position. Then she set up a tray over his lap.

He looked at the food without interest. 'I'm really not hungry.'

'Try to eat a little,' she urged him.

Without any enthusiasm, and mainly just to get rid of this perky girl, he picked up a piece of toast and took a bite. The girl smiled with approval and left. He took another bite, and to his surprise, he managed to get both slices down. Moments later, an orderly came in with a basin. Ken suffered through a sponge bath, but at least he was allowed to brush his own teeth. A nurse appeared with some pills for him to take. The pain went away, but he stayed awake. And he actually began to feel almost human.

He must have looked almost human too, because when his parents arrived they seemed very relieved to see him. His mother began to prattle about the doctor's report, how Ken could probably come home tomorrow or the next day, as soon as he learned how to manoeuvre some crutches, but his father was oddly silent. And even as his mother continued to prattle, Ken sensed something behind her determinedly cheerful expression.

'What's the matter?' he asked.

His parents looked at each other.

'Is Jack in worse shape than me? Is he going to play tonight?'

His father took his hand. 'Son . . . you have to be strong. We have something difficult to tell you.'

Ken had a terrible feeling he knew what they were about to say. That he'd never play soccer again. He steeled himself to deal with it.

'What is it, Dad?'

'Jack didn't make it, Ken. He died.'

Ken hadn't prepared himself for that.

He couldn't remember the last time he'd cried in front of his parents. Probably not since he was five or six. But he felt absolutely no shame in crying now. Jack was his best friend, they'd been buddies since they were little kids. And now he was gone.

His parents stayed with him and tried to comfort him. Then a nurse came in to give him another shot.

'This will help you sleep,' she said.

He didn't want to sleep. He wanted to think about Jack. He wanted to stay awake and ask questions. Why had Jack died and he'd survived? Was he to blame for the collision? But the medication was stronger than he was.

Much later, he opened his eyes to a room that was still dark. He could just make out the flowers and balloons that friends and family had sent. He was alone, and he was glad to be alone, because now he had a chance to think.

What happened? How did it happen? Had Jack suffered? And where was Jack now . . .

He hadn't spoken out loud and he didn't expect an answer, but he got one.

I'm here.

He didn't see anyone, but he'd know that voice anywhere. 'Jack?'

Yeah, it's me.

Relief flooded over him. 'So you're not dead.'

Oh, I'm dead, all right. Bummer, huh?

So this was a dream. It had to be a dream. Ken didn't believe in ghosts.

In case you're wondering, it wasn't anyone's fault. You

know how I never learned to fall right. I broke my neck.
I guess that's the way the cookie crumbles.

'You didn't deserve to die,' Ken murmured.

Whatever. Anyway, just thought you'd like to know, it
wasn't your fault.

'OK. Thanks for telling me.'

What a weird dream, Ken thought. I've never had
one like this before. It feels so real.

This isn't a dream.

'How'd you know what I was thinking?'

I don't know. I just did. I can't explain. I'm not really
talking either. I mean, dead people don't talk, do we? I
don't know — it's like you and I are communicating with
our minds.

'Oh. I don't get it.'

Look, I don't understand it either. But it's kind of cool,
huh?

'Yeah, I guess.'

You must be tired.

'Yeah, kind of.'

Go back to sleep. We'll talk later.

'Right.'

Jack's voice faded away and another dream began.

This one was a lot easier to deal with. He was a judge in a Miss California beauty pageant. Blondes in bikinis sauntered past him. They were all gorgeous, and he had no idea how he'd pick out the prettiest.

When he opened his eyes again, that perky girl in the pink pinafore was in his room. 'Have a nice nap?' she chirped. 'It's lunchtime.' Once again, she set up a tray on his bed.

He watched as she left the room. Actually, she was kind of cute. Not like the Miss California beauties, of course.

Yeah, I know what you mean. Those California girls — man, they were hot! *There was this one on the beach — I know you'll think I'm bragging, but I swear she was looking at me . . .*

That was when Ken had to accept the fact that his conversation with Jack wasn't a dream.

It was a nightmare, and it was just beginning.

CHAPTER THREE

A MANDA WAS USUALLY PRETTY good at hiding her feelings. She'd learned from several bad experiences not to let herself care too much about other people and their problems. And when she felt sorry for herself, or depressed, or angry, or anything like that, she didn't let it show. She was Amanda Beeson, Queen Bee, the prettiest, best-dressed and most envied girl at Meadowbrook Middle School. She had a reputation to uphold. And feeling sorry for yourself was so not cool.

So throughout the rest of the class, she kept her face fixed in what was a normal expression for her: mildly bored and generally uninterested in anything going on around her. She would *not* let anyone in this class see how annoyed she was. How they'd hurt her feelings.

Maybe she shouldn't think that 'they' had done anything – after all, it was only Jenna who had really insulted her. But the rest of them had laughed, so they were just as guilty.

How *dare* Jenna suggest that her gift was worthless? *Nothing* about Amanda Beeson was worthless. As for her gift – she was a bodysnatcher, for crying out loud! Jenna could read minds – big deal. Emily could tell the future – so what? Amanda could become another person! And they all knew it.

In this very class, she'd taken over three of them at different times. Tracey, Ken, Sarah – they'd all had personal experience of Amanda's bodysnatching skills. They knew how talented she was, and they should respect her for it. They should have defended her against Jenna's attack.

In all honesty, she had to acknowledge (but only to herself) that she didn't have complete control of her talent. In fact, circumstances often forced her to snatch bodies she didn't want. Like the time when she felt sorry for Tracey Devon, who used to be so pathetic. Who would want to be in Tracey Devon's body?

But Amanda had ended up there, and that was *not* fun. She still had to feel sorry for someone to become that person, but it was getting easier. She could always find something to pity about a person. After all, they all had the misfortune of not being Amanda Beeson.

But while she was very sure that most of the girls at Meadowbrook looked up to her, did any of her classmates in this class realize how superior she was? She suspected that they didn't. They probably agreed with Jenna. None of them thought she'd be any help in a dangerous situation. And that was so not true. Had Emily forgotten how Amanda-as-Tracey helped her escape from that insane student teacher? And didn't Ken remember how she'd dealt with one of his voices?

She remembered that experience all too well. The guy's name was Rick, he was a teenager who'd died in the 1960s, and he was lonely. He bothered Ken incessantly. And when Amanda took over Ken's body, Rick talked to *her*. It didn't bother her so much though, mainly because she'd fallen in love with Rick.

Ken didn't know about that, of course. All he knew was that somehow Amanda had managed to persuade Rick to leave him alone. And he should be grateful to her for it. Not to mention how she'd transformed Tracey's entire life. That was worth recalling, wasn't it?

As far as she was concerned, she'd done a lot of good for a lot of people with her gift. How could they treat her like this?

Well, they were going to regret it, and soon. Because she was about to make an announcement that would stun them all and make them feel terrible guilt for teasing her.

She'd planned to tell them earlier in the class, but Madame wouldn't let her. The teacher had gone on and on about their enemies and the danger they were in and all that boring stuff. But there was one thing she knew for sure about Madame – she was courteous and she was fair. She'd give Amanda her opportunity.

Sure enough, when Madame finally finished nagging them, she remembered that she had cut Amanda off earlier.

'Amanda, you said you had something on your mind. Would you like to share it with us?'

Amanda composed herself. She sat up straight and lowered her eyes. And she spoke quietly.

'This is very hard for me to talk about.'

Madame actually seemed concerned. 'Go on, Amanda. You're among friends here.'

Ha! Amanda thought. But she took a deep breath and spoke solemnly.

'I wanted to let you all know that I'm going to be out of class for a few days.' She paused dramatically. 'You see, I'm going into hospital.'

She was rewarded with a satisfying gasp. Emily looked positively stricken. Tracey had her hand to her mouth, and even Jenna was taken aback.

'What's wrong with you?' Charles asked.

Before she could answer, Madame spoke. 'Yes, I've had a note from your mother. You're having your tonsils out.'

There was a moment of silence. Then Jenna spoke. 'Is that all?'

Amanda drew herself up stiffly. 'What do you mean by that?'

Jenna shrugged. 'Everyone gets their tonsils out. Well, maybe not *everyone*. But it's no big deal. I mean, it's common.'

'It's still an operation,' Amanda stated hotly. 'OK, maybe little kids have it all the time, but it's more serious when you're older.'

At least, Madame backed her up. 'Amanda's right. And any stay in a hospital is distressing. We'll miss you in class, Amanda, and we all wish you a speedy recovery. Martin, are you all right?'

Martin was having one of his coughing fits. 'Someone must have been eating peanut butter in the cafeteria,' he managed to croak.

Everyone knew that Martin was allergic to peanut butter. He couldn't even smell it without getting sick. Madame hastened to his side. 'Come along, Martin, I'm taking you to the infirmary.'

Amanda couldn't believe it. Martin's stupid allergies were considered more important than her tonsils?

Just as Madame was leaving the room with Martin, the bell rang. Ever since Meadowbrook's reorganization of the class schedule a couple of weeks ago, this class had been moved from just after lunch to the last period of the day. Amanda was pleased with this. The Gifted class always put her in a weird mood, and it was a relief to know she could join her real friends immediately afterwards and get out of there.

Normally Amanda would be up and out of there very quickly. But this time there was an odd, burning sensation in her eyes, and she stayed in her seat. There was no way she would let anyone see her cry.

Her classmates ran out without a word to her. Except for one. Ken paused by her desk.

'Hey, sorry to hear about that.'

Her urge to cry vanished. 'What?'

'It's no fun being in the hospital. I know all about that.'

She knew he'd been in hospital for a while after an accident earlier in the school year. 'You understand how I feel,' she said softly.

He nodded. 'You must be scared.'

'I am,' she said, and she was actually being honest. She got up, gathered her things, and they left the room together.

'There's nothing to be scared about,' he assured

her as they walked downstairs. 'The nurses and doctors, they're really nice. The worst thing about it is being bored. Bring magazines and books. And make sure your parents arrange for you to have a TV in your room.'

'OK.' On the ground floor he turned in the opposite direction from her locker, but she didn't care. She continued walking by his side.

'But you probably won't have to worry about being bored. You'll get a lot of visitors.'

She gave him a sidelong glance. 'Really? Do you think so?'

'Well, you've got lots of friends, haven't you?'

'Oh, sure. But not in our class.'

She was disappointed when he didn't pick up on the hint. She had a thing for Ken ever since he'd kissed her at her friend Sophie's pool party the previous August. She knew that kiss didn't mean anything serious – all the boys were daring each other to do stupid things, like throwing a particular person in the pool or outdoing each other in the number of somersaults they could perform while diving. Silly stuff like that.

But she remembered the kiss. And when she'd been placed in the so-called 'gifted' class, the one thing that had lifted her spirits was the fact that Ken was there.

She had to keep this conversation going. 'Did you hear what Jenna said about me in class?'

Ken looked apologetic. 'I wasn't really listening.'

She knew what that meant – dead people had been talking to him. But she also knew that he didn't like talking about his gift.

'What did Jenna say?' he asked.

'She was talking about my gift. She said it was worthless. I know she thinks I couldn't help anyone if we were in danger.'

'That's not true!' Ken exclaimed. 'You could help.' He considered it for a second. 'For example, you could take over the body of an enemy and stop that person from doing bad things.'

There was no way on earth that Amanda would want to do something like that, but she didn't tell him that.

Ken went on. 'It's *my* gift that's worthless. At least, it's useless in a crisis.'

'I don't believe that,' Amanda said stoutly, before it occurred to her that she couldn't think of one possible situation when talking to dead people could help anyone out of a dangerous predicament. 'You have a wonderful gift,' she said anyway, hoping he wouldn't ask her to elaborate.

'Oh, yeah? What good is it?'

Thinking rapidly, she said, 'Um, well, you could bring loved ones together. Maybe there's someone who's desperate to connect with a dead husband or something.'

'Yeah, I get requests like that all the time,' he admitted. 'But I'll tell you something . . .' He stopped walking and looked at her. 'This is really awful. But I really don't want to get involved in their lives. Is that terrible of me?'

She could have kissed him right there and then. 'No, it's not terrible! I understand completely. It's not like we can solve everyone's problems. I mean, we all have our own problems to deal with, right?'

He gave her a half-smile, and her heart was full. They were bonding!

They'd reached his locker. As he twisted the

combination, she considered the possibilities. Would he walk with her to her locker now? Maybe he'd ask her to have a Coke with him at the mall across the street. If not, maybe she could invite him back to her place. But what could she use for an excuse? They didn't have any other classes together – she couldn't pretend to need homework help.

Then she noticed he was frowning. In his hand, he held a piece of paper.

'What's that?'

'I'm not sure. I just found it on the floor of my locker.'

He showed it to her.

It was an announcement. Or maybe invitation was a better word.

SEANCE.

That was the word all in capital letters on the top. Underneath, it read:

Make contact with those who have passed on. Connect with your loved ones. Ask questions, get answers.

There was an address, a date – today's date – and a time, eight p.m. On the bottom, someone had scrawled the words: *Ken, are you one of us? Would you like to meet others who have your gift?*

There was no signature, no name. Amanda looked at Ken. All the colour had drained from his face.

'Where did this come from?' she asked.

'I don't know.'

'Someone must have slipped it through the locker slot,' Amanda said. 'Maybe it's a joke from someone in our class.'

Ken shook his head. 'I don't think so.'

She had to agree with him. Their classmates didn't pull pranks.

'Does anyone else know about your gift?' she asked.

'No.'

'You don't have any idea who could have put that in your locker?'

'No.' He stuffed the note in his pocket. 'I gotta go. See ya.'

And to her disappointment, he slammed the locker door closed and strode down the hall.

CHAPTER FOUR

WHAT KEN HAD SAID to Amanda wasn't really true. He had a very good idea who could have left that note in his locker. Because there *was* someone outside of the gifted class who knew what he could do.

Outside the building, the note still in his hand, he paused by a rubbish bin. A friend who lived in his neighbourhood waved to him. 'Hey, Preston, my brother's picking me up. Want a ride home?'

'No, thanks,' Ken called back. 'I'm not leaving yet. I've got a couple of things to do.' He was about to toss the paper in the bin, but instead he stuck the crumpled note in his pocket and took off.

Actually, he felt like thinking and he needed to be alone for that. He headed around to the back of the canteen, where there was a bench under a tree, and sat down. Much as he didn't enjoy reliving the past, he was going to have to let his mind wander back to those days after the accident.

He was allowed to go home three days after he regained consciousness. His parents came for him. Even though he had his crutches now, hospital regulations insisted he leave in a wheelchair. His parents followed as a nurse wheeled him out into the car park.

'Happy to be going home, Ken?' the nurse chirped cheerfully.

'Yes,' Ken replied. What a stupid question, he thought. Of course he was glad to be going back to his own bed, his mother's cooking . . . and maybe an end to those disturbing conversations with his dead friend.

It was just so – so strange, having Jack in his head. It didn't feel right. But what could he do? His best friend was dead. The least he could do was listen to him.

Grabbing his crutches, he got out of the wheel-chair and hobbled into the car. As his parents got in, he noticed for the first time that they were very dressed up for a weekday afternoon. His mother wore heels and a black dress with a small strand of pearls at her neck. His father wore a dark suit with a white shirt and black tie.

'Where are you going?' he asked them.

His parents exchanged meaningful looks. 'It's where we've been,' his mother told him gently. 'Jack's funeral was this morning.'

'Oh.'

'Later, we're going to his home to pay a condolence call,' she went on.

'I guess I should go too,' Ken said.

'If you like, you can come with us,' his mother said.

'But we'll understand if you don't feel up to it,' his father added.

He knew he should go. He'd known Jack's family for a long time. But all he could think about right now was the way they'd probably look at him. He was alive and their son was dead. Maybe they would even hold him responsible for the collision.

He could get out of it – he knew that. All he had

to do was say he felt tired, or that his ribs hurt. And that was what he planned to do. Someday, maybe in a week or two, he would stop by and see them. Apologize. It was the least he could do.

His father helped him out of the car while his mother adjusted his crutches. He winced as he limped into the house, keenly aware of the dull ache in his chest from the broken ribs. Slowly, he managed to get down the hall and into his bedroom. His mother fussed over him, adjusting his pillow, bringing magazines, asking if he was hungry.

'I had your prescription filled, so tell me if you're in pain,' she said.

At the same time, another voice spoke.

Hey, Ken. Can you talk?

His heart sank. But what could he say? 'Sure.'

He didn't realize he'd spoken out loud until his mother came closer. 'Here are the pills, and I'll get you some water.'

'I'm not in pain,' Ken said.

His mother looked confused.

Ken? Are you there? I gotta ask you something.

'Wait a second.'

Now his mother was concerned. 'Ken, are you all right?'

'I'm fine, I'm fine,' Ken said quickly. 'I – I think I'm going to sleep a while.'

His mother gave him one more worried look, and finally left the room.

Ken sat up and listened. Was Jack still there?

Yeah, I'm here.

That was when he realized he didn't have to speak out loud to communicate with Jack. He only had to direct his thoughts.

I've got a favour to ask you.

What?

It's about Lucy.

What about her?

I bought her this gift, from California. It's a bracelet made out of seashells. I was going to give it to her the day I got back, but we had a fight.

What about?

Stupid stuff. I kept talking about the cute girls on the beach in California, and she got jealous.

What do you want me to do?

Could you give her the bracelet? It's in the top drawer

of my desk, in my bedroom. And . . . and tell her I'm sorry about the fight. She'll understand. Will you do that for me?

Yeah, OK. Hey, Jack . . .

What?

What's it like, where you are?

It's OK. I can't really describe it — you wouldn't understand. I'll check with you tomorrow and find out what Lucy said, OK?

Tomorrow? Ken thought in alarm. I have to do it by tomorrow?

But there was no response. Jack was gone. Ken sank back on his pillow and wished he could make some sense out of this. He'd always been a pretty down-to-earth guy. Sure, he enjoyed psycho-thriller movies as much as any of his friends did, but he'd never been really scared by them because he didn't believe in that spooky stuff.

He still didn't believe in it. So how could he explain hearing Jack's voice? Was he just imagining these conversations? Had his brain been damaged in the accident? The doctor had said all the tests and scans were fine, but doctors could make mistakes.

Only he *felt* fine too except for the pain in his ribs and his ankle. His head didn't hurt at all. And he couldn't have been imagining Jack's voice. It was just too real.

So now what? He had to find the bracelet Jack told him about. Deliver it to Lucy. And tell her Jack was sorry.

Would Lucy think he'd lost his mind? Possibly. He didn't really care though. He'd never told Jack this, but Lucy wasn't one of his favourite people in the world. He'd always thought she was kind of shallow – one of those girls who only thinks about herself. The kind of girl who was accustomed to always getting what she wanted. Having seen her flirt with other guys at school, he'd wondered how much she really cared about Jack. But Jack liked her, so Ken had to be nice to her.

The truth of it was, he had to do this for Jack, whether he wanted to or not. He got off his bed and went to the door.

'Mom? When you and Dad go to the Farrells' – could you let me know? I'd like to go with you.'

As Ken had expected, the scene at the Farrell house was pretty grim. There was a black wreath on the door. Jack's mother, her eyes red, hugged him, and Jack's father put an arm around him. Neither of them acted like Ken was responsible for Jack's death, and Ken was ashamed for even thinking they might.

There were other people at the house too – Jack's friends from school and other adults who were neighbours and friends. A lot of people brought food, and the big dining room table was covered with cakes and pies. It could have been a party, except that there was no music, no laughing. And no one was having a good time.

Ken chatted quietly with a couple of friends, but all the time he was thinking about how and when he could get into Jack's bedroom. Should he come up with an excuse? He could say he wanted to get the tennis racket he'd loaned to Jack. But that would sound kind of cruel, like he was afraid he'd never get the racket back now that Jack was dead. Maybe he could say he wanted to borrow a book, but that didn't seem right either. Jack wasn't much of a reader.

It might be best just to sneak into the room. There were plenty of other people there – no one would notice if he went missing for a little while. And there was a bathroom right next to Jack's bedroom – he could say he was going there if anyone asked.

In the end, he didn't have to invent an excuse. Jack's father took him aside.

'Ken, you were Jack's best friend, and we'd like you to have something to remember him by. When you have a chance, go into his room and choose something – anything. His jacket, maybe. Or the karate trophy. Whatever you want.'

Ken nodded. 'Thank you, Mr Farrell.'

On his crutches, he hobbled down the hall to Jack's room. Once inside, he closed the door, and went over to Jack's desk. Just as Jack had told him, the seashell bracelet was in the top drawer. He shoved it into his pocket.

But what if Mr Farrell wanted to see the souvenir he'd chosen? He looked around the room. There was a stack of old comic books on a shelf. He and Jack had been Spider-Man fanatics when they were little kids. He took an issue off the pile, and left the room.

When he returned to the living room, he saw that some people had left and others had arrived. And among the new arrivals was Lucy. He stood back and watched her for a while.

He had to admit, for a pretty girl she looked pretty awful. Her normally pale face was even paler than usual, and there were dark shadows under her red eyes. Clearly, she'd been crying a lot and hadn't had much sleep. So maybe he'd been wrong about her feelings for Jack. She certainly looked grief-stricken, like someone who'd lost the love of her life, and his heart ached for her.

He adjusted his crutches and limped over to her.

'Hi, Lucy.'

She managed a small, woebegone smile. 'Hi, Ken. How are you feeling?'

'OK. How are you?'

She shrugged. 'Well, you know . . .'

'Yeah. I know. Look, Lucy, I need to talk to you. It's kind of personal.' He glanced around. The room was getting crowded, and he didn't want anyone else hearing what he had to say. 'Um, do you want to go outside for a minute? Get some air?'

She followed him through the kitchen and out the back door. Fortunately, there was no one else in the back garden.

But how to begin? How was he going to tell this unbelievable tale?

'I know how awful this must be for you,' he said.

'Tell me about it,' Lucy said. 'You know, Ken, this was going to be the best year of my life. Jack was the coolest guy I ever went out with. I mean, he was cute, he was vice-captain of the soccer team . . . all my girlfriends were jealous. I'd already bought a dress to wear for the eighth-grade dance . . .' A tear trickled down her cheek. 'I can't believe this happened to me.'

'You could still go to the dance,' he said, and immediately wanted to bite his tongue. What a lame thing to say.

She sighed. 'With who?'

He thought she probably meant something like she wouldn't want to go with anyone but Jack.

'I still don't understand how he died,' she murmured. 'He just fell down.' She looked up. 'You crashed into him, right?'

'Well, we sort of crashed into each other,' Ken said.

'But you're not dead.'

He bit his lower lip. 'I'm really sorry, Lucy.'

'Sorry you're not dead?'

'Well, no, but . . .'

'Sorry you didn't look where you were going?'

Ken felt sick. 'Lucy, I don't think it was my fault. The coach, the doctor – everyone said it was an accident.'

She shrugged. 'Whatever.'

'Jack doesn't blame me,' he blurted out, needing to convince her he wasn't in the wrong.

'How do you know?' she asked sharply.

This wasn't how he'd wanted to bring it up. But he had to tell her sooner or later. 'Because . . . because he told me.'

Her eyebrows went up. 'Before he died?'

'No. After.'

She stared at him for a moment. 'I don't understand.'

'Neither do I,' Ken admitted. He took a deep

breath. 'Lucy, I know this is going to sound pretty bizarre, but . . . Jack's been talking to me.'

Her eyes widened. 'You mean – you've seen his ghost?'

'No, it's not like that. I hear his voice. In my head.'

She blinked. 'He – he contacted you from beyond the grave?'

Ken nodded. 'He started talking to me while I was in the hospital. I don't understand it – maybe it's because we collided, but . . . he's able to talk with me. I know this sounds totally crazy . . .'

Lucy gazed at him thoughtfully. 'Not really. Lots of people believe in stuff like that. My mother went to a medium once. Do you know what a medium is?'

'No.'

'It's someone who's in contact with the spirit world. My mother said the medium put her in touch with her great-great-grandfather.' She smiled. 'There'd always been a rumour in the family that he'd buried some treasure during the Civil War. She wanted to know where it was.'

'Did she find out?'

Lucy shook her head. 'It turned out to be a legend. Too bad, huh?'

'That's . . . interesting,' Ken said.

'What did Jack tell you?' she asked. 'Did he say anything about me?'

'Yeah. He wanted me to give you this.' He reached in his pocket and pulled out the bracelet. 'He got it for you in California.'

'Oh, wow!' Lucy exclaimed. 'It's really cute.' She put the bracelet on. 'How does it look?'

'Fine,' Ken said quickly. 'And he wanted me to tell you he was sorry about that argument you guys had just after he came back from California.'

'OK.' She admired the bracelet on her arm. 'At least now I have something to remember him by. Thanks, Ken.'

'You're welcome.'

'And if you talk to Jack again, tell him . . . tell him I forgive him. About the fight.'

'OK, I will.'

'I want to go and show off the bracelet to my friends,' she said, and turned to go back to the house.

'Lucy, wait!'

She turned back. 'What?'

'Um, listen, you can't tell anyone how I knew about the bracelet. How Jack's been talking to me. Everyone will think I'm nuts.'

Lucy nodded. 'You're probably right. I mean, people just aren't very open-minded about this kind of thing. Don't worry, I'll say Jack mailed it to me from California and it just arrived today.'

'Thanks a lot,' Ken said fervently.

She smiled, cocked her head to one side and gazed at him oddly, like she was scrutinizing him or judging him. Which wasn't surprising, Ken thought, considering what she'd just learned about him. Then, without saying anything else, she ran back into the house.

When Ken went back inside, he was grateful to find his parents ready to leave. He said his goodbyes to the Farrells, and once he was in the car he told his parents he was really tired so they wouldn't talk to him.

What a relief to have that over with! Now he could give Jack an honest report. He'd given Lucy the bracelet, apologized on Jack's behalf, and Lucy had seemed pleased with the gift. Maybe . . . maybe this would put an end to Jack's communication.

And then he felt terrible. Jack was *dead*. The least Ken could do for him was listen. Maybe he'd get used to it. He'd *have* to get used to it. He could never tell his best friend to stop talking to him.

He really was tired, he realized when he got home. Once in bed he considered taking a sleeping pill, but he figured he was so wiped out he'd fall asleep without one.

Ken?

Oh, no. Jack wasn't supposed to contact him till tomorrow.

I'm kind of tired right now, Jack.

What did you call me? My name isn't Jack.

Ken frowned.

Who is this?

I'm Arthur. Arthur Penfield. I'm dead. And I was wondering if you could get a message to my brother.

Ken sat up, his heart pounding furiously.

Wait a minute — you've got the wrong guy. I don't know anyone named Arthur Penfield.

No, we've never met. I died before you were born.

Then – why are you contacting me? Talk to one of your own friends!

None of my friends have your gift. You're one in a million, son. You're going to be hearing from a lot of us.

Suddenly, Ken didn't feel very well. What was this Arthur guy talking about? What gift?

'Leave me alone!'

He didn't realize he'd spoken out loud until his door opened.

'What's wrong, Ken?' his mother asked. 'Darling, you're sweating! We shouldn't have let you come with us tonight. It was too soon for you to be out and about.' Worriedly, she put a hand on his forehead.

Oh, if only he could blame this on a fever! If only he could tell her what was happening. Yeah, right. He'd be back in a hospital before dawn. And possibly in a straitjacket.

'I'm not feeling so great, Mom,' was all he could say. 'Could I have one of those pills now?'

He wasn't actually in any pain. He was just hoping the pill might put him to sleep immediately. Because he didn't really want to hear from any more dead people tonight. Or ever again.

But he had a very, very bad feeling about this. He didn't think there was any kind of pill that was going to put an end to these strange communications.

CHAPTER FIVE

IN THE MONTHS THAT followed the accident and Jack's death, Ken didn't see much of Lucy. She was a year younger, in the eighth grade, so they didn't have any classes together. And fortunately, since Meadowbrook was a pretty big school, you didn't run into the same people every day in the hallways. If he did run into her and they made eye contact, they just mumbled vague greetings. She never asked him any more questions about Jack, and he suspected that she didn't think much about her late boyfriend.

But she was the only one, outside of his gifted classmates, who had been told about his 'gift'. And so, after getting his thoughts together, he went in search of her.

He remembered that Lucy was a cheerleader and he knew that the cheerleaders practised almost every day after classes were finished, so he headed to the gym. When he got there, the cheerleaders had just started to gather. He spotted Lucy outside the gym entrance, talking to Simon Dowell. Simon was on the soccer team, but Ken had never known him very well.

He ambled towards them. 'Hi, guys.'

'Yo, Preston,' Simon muttered. He didn't look too thrilled to see Ken. But Lucy didn't seem to mind the interruption.

'Hi, Ken!'

He tried to sound casual. 'Lucy, can I talk to you for a second?'

'Sure!'

Ken glanced at Simon. 'Um, it's kind of personal.' He hated saying that – he knew it made him sound secretive and mysterious – but he couldn't talk about Jack in front of Simon.

Lucy looked surprised and Simon was clearly annoyed. Ken realized Simon must have been flirting with Lucy, and he groaned inwardly. Now Simon would think Ken was trying to make a play for her.

'It's about a class,' he added quickly, which was another stupid thing to say since he had no classes with Lucy. But Lucy actually smiled.

'Excuse me, Simon,' she said, and moved away. Ken followed her to a relatively private corner of the gym.

Lucy smiled prettily. 'What's up, Ken?'

Ken took the crumpled paper from his pocket, and unfolded it. 'I was wondering if you know anything about this.'

Lucy took the paper. 'Seance,' she read out loud.

'Shh!' Ken hissed. He glanced around nervously. 'Just read it to yourself, OK?'

She did. From the way her brow furrowed as she read, Ken knew this was the first time she'd seen the announcement.

'I don't get it,' she said. 'Why are you showing me this?'

'Well, you're the only one I ever told about Jack talking to me. So I thought, maybe, well . . . you might have put this in my locker. Because you thought I'd be interested.'

She looked at him blankly for a second, and then

her expression cleared. 'Oh, right. You told me Jack talked to you after he died, didn't you?'

'He told me to give you the bracelet, remember?'

'I remember. Do you still talk to Jack?'

'Once in a while.'

'How's he doing?'

'He's all right. I mean, considering the fact that he's dead.'

Lucy nodded. 'It's funny — back when you first told me about that, I thought you'd just imagined Jack talking to you. I mean, you'd had a concussion, hadn't you?'

'Yeah.'

'But it's for real,' she said thoughtfully. 'What do you and Jack talk about?'

He was beginning to feel even more uncomfortable. 'Stuff. So, you didn't give me this announcement about the seance?'

She shook her head. 'Sounds cool though. Can I come?'

'Um, I don't even know if I'm going.' He crumpled the paper and stuck it back in his pocket. 'See ya, Lucy.'

'Wait!' Lucy called.

'What?'

'Tell Jack I said "hi", OK?'

'Yeah, sure.'

Ken hurried off, feeling frustrated. So Lucy hadn't slipped this note in his locker. Then who? At home in his room, he put the crumpled paper on his desk and smoothed it out.

SEANCE.

Could someone from his gifted class have put it in his locker? But why wouldn't that person just tell him?

Ken, are you one of us? Would you like to meet others who have your gift?

Madame was always saying there were other people who knew about them. Bad people. But maybe they weren't *all* bad. And maybe, just maybe, there really were other people out there who had this ability to communicate with the dead.

He had to wonder – did it bother them as much as it bothered him? How did they deal with it? Could they offer any advice on how to control it? He was pretty sure by now that he'd never be able to get rid of it, but maybe there was a way to turn it on and off.

He wouldn't have any problem getting out of the house tonight. It was a Friday, and it wasn't unusual for him to go out, joining some friends who went to the bowling alley practically every Friday night. He glanced at the address on the announcement. This place wasn't far from the bowling alley. He wouldn't even have to lie to his parents really – he could stop by the alley on his way back from the seance.

His mobile phone rang. 'Hello?'

'Hi Ken, this is Amanda.'

For reasons of safety, in case they got into trouble, Madame had insisted that all members of the gifted class exchange phone numbers. But he'd never had a call from Amanda before.

'Ken, are you there?'

'Oh sure. I'm sorry, I guess I was daydreaming.'

'The voices?' Amanda asked sympathetically.

'You know how it is,' he mumbled. She really did too, because of that brief period when she'd taken over his body. He still felt a little embarrassed when he thought about it.

'What's up?'

'I was just wondering . . . are you going to that seance tonight?'

'I'm kind of thinking about it,' Ken admitted.

'Would you like some company?'

He was surprised. 'You?'

'Yes,' she replied. 'And you'd be doing me a favour. I'm a little nervous about going into the hospital on Sunday. I'm trying to keep busy so I won't think about it.'

Ken considered it. He'd actually been feeling a little warmer towards Amanda lately. She seemed less snobby than she used to be, more interesting. And earlier today, when they'd talked about their gifts, he almost felt like they understood each other.

Hey man, what's going on?

It was Jack. Hang on a sec, Ken told him, and spoke into the phone.

'OK. I'll come to your house and collect you at seven thirty.'

After he hung up, he wondered if maybe he should have told her to meet him somewhere. Picking her up at her house made this seem almost like a date.

You've got a date? Who with?

He'd forgotten Jack was there.

Amanda Beeson, he replied. *Only it's not really a date. We're just going to the same place.*

But I heard you — you said you'd pick her up at home. That makes it a date.

Ken grinned.

Well, maybe that's not so terrible . . .

I had a feeling you guys would hook up eventually. Where are ya going?

To a seance. Where people try to make contact with the dead.

He could hear Jack chortle. *You're kidding. You believe in that garbage?*

I just thought it might be interesting.

Yeah, OK. Hey, you seen Lucy lately?

Yes, today. In the gym.

Even from beyond the grave, he could hear the wistfulness in Jack's tone.

Is she hanging out with anyone?

I'm not sure. I think maybe Simon Dowell is into her.

Simon Dowell? That scumbag?

Why do you call him a scumbag?

Don't you know his reputation? I used to think he was making up the stories he used to tell about all the girls he's been with, but maybe it's true. Anyway, I don't want him messing around Lucy — he's bad news.

There's not much you can do about it, Ken pointed out.

Yeah, I know. But you *could.*

Ken's heart sank. *What do you mean?*

Could you keep an eye on her? Distract her?

And how am I supposed to do that? Jack, you don't want me *to hook up with* Lucy?

No, no, nothing like that. Be kind of a big brother to her. Just — just hang out with her a little. Let her know what a jerk Dowell is. C'mon, Ken, do this for me. Please?

OK, OK.

And don't let her know I put you up to this! She'll think I'm jealous and it'll just make her more conceited.

Yeah, yeah, whatever. Listen, I've got to go — we'll talk later.

Jack 'hung up', or whatever it was he did to cut the communication. Ken flopped down in a chair. Now what? Would he really have to hang out with

Lucy? He supposed it wouldn't be the end of the world, to get together with her once or twice and warn her off Simon Dowell. But what if Amanda saw him with Lucy?

He had to smile. Amanda wouldn't care, would she? It wasn't like they had a relationship.

Not yet.

The address for the seance turned out to be an apartment building. Examining the announcement again, Ken saw that there was a number next to the address – forty-six.

'I guess this must be the apartment number,' he told Amanda.

Amanda was looking at the list of names next to buttons outside the front entrance. 'There's no name next to forty-six.'

Ken pressed the button. He expected to hear a voice asking him to identify himself. Instead, a buzzer indicated that the door had been unlocked.

Silently, they went inside. To the left of the entranceway, there was a lift. Inside, buttons were labelled one to five. Ken pressed four.

The lift doors opened on a hallway. They didn't have to look at the numbers on the doors to find number forty-six – one of them opened immediately.

The figure inside the door spoke sweetly. 'Welcome. You may enter.'

Ken felt Amanda take his hand, and he couldn't blame her. The woman looked very unusual. She wore a long, flowing robe, dark green with little golden sparkly things all over it. Over her head was some kind of veil – layers of silky stuff – and it completely covered her face. Tiny slits gave her the ability to see them, but they couldn't make out her face at all.

They went inside the apartment. The interior wasn't as spooky as its inhabitant. There was a living-room area, with a sofa and a couple of armchairs. Just off the living room was the dining area with a round table, but it wasn't being used for dining at the moment. Three people were sitting there – two women and a boy. Ken didn't recognize any of them.

'Join us,' the veiled woman said as she went over to the table. There were three empty chairs. Ken took the seat next to the boy and Amanda sat beside one of the women. Then the veiled woman sat down.

'I am Cassandra,' she said. 'I am your medium. You will talk to me, and I will attempt to reach the spirits you wish to contact. But I must warn you, your first attempt at contact may not be successful. It takes effort and practice to communicate with the spirit world. You must be determined and you must be patient. Much depends on the need and willingness of your loved one in the spirit world to speak to you. They may need to be convinced, and I will try to convince them. But there are no guarantees.'

Amanda spoke. 'Will we get our money back if we can't make contact?'

The woman turned towards her. 'Have I asked you for any money? I do not charge for my work. That would be wrong. I have a gift, and it is my responsibility and obligation to share this gift freely.'

That was interesting, Ken thought. So this seance thing wasn't a scam. Maybe this medium, Cassandra, could actually do what he could do. The only difference was that she probably had more control of her gift. And she seemed to be pleased to have it.

'Before we begin attempting contact,' she continued, 'we need to establish a connection among ourselves. Each of you will introduce yourself, and explain what you hope to accomplish here.' She turned to Amanda. 'You may begin. What is your name?'

'I'm Amanda.' She hesitated. 'Do I have to give my last name too?'

'No, that won't be necessary – not if you don't want to,' the medium said smoothly. 'We respect each other's privacy here. Why have you come to the seance, Amanda? What do you hope to accomplish?'

Ken looked at his classmate worriedly. Had she guessed she would have to say something? What would happen if she told them she just came to keep him company? Would she be thrown out?

But Amanda was cool. 'I've been thinking about my great-grandmother lately. I'd like to talk to her.'

'For any particular reason?' the medium asked.

'Well, I never knew her – she died before I was born – and I just want to say "hi".'

Ken gave his name. 'Um, there's no one in particular I'm trying to reach. I was just wondering if any of my ancestors wanted to contact me.'

The medium appeared to accept that. 'All right.' She turned to the woman who was sitting next to Amanda. 'And you are . . . ?'

'Margaret.' She spoke barely above a whisper. 'I want to talk to my mother.' There was a catch in her voice.

Ken looked at her. She wasn't very old – just in her twenties, he'd guess. Which meant her mother must have died young. She certainly looked depressed. She had long, limp brown hair, with a fringe that hung over the thick brown-framed glasses that covered her eyes. She was pasty-pale.

The medium must have picked up on the sadness in her tone. She responded gently.

'Did you lose your mother recently, Margaret?'

'Yes. She died only two weeks ago. I – I miss her so much!'

'I understand,' the medium said. 'I hope we'll be able to reach her. Next?'

The woman sitting by Margaret looked completely different. First of all, she didn't seem miserable at all. Her heavily made-up green eyes sparkled, and her face was framed by carefully styled silver-grey curls. Long dangly loops hung from her ears, and she wore an orange shawl over a purple dress.

'I'm Dahlia,' she said brightly. 'At least, that's my name *now*. I believe this is my fourth life, but it may be my fifth. In my previous reincarnations I've been called Maria, Constance, Genevieve—'

The medium interrupted her. 'Yes, well, we'll call you by your current name. Why are you here, Dahlia?'

'Well, my memory isn't what it used to be,' the woman said. 'And I don't want to forget all the friends I've made in my other lives. I'd like to make contact with them and reminisce about old times.'

'But how do you know they're in the spirit world?' the medium asked. 'Perhaps, like you, they've been reincarnated too.'

Dahlia shook her head. 'No, very few people are

like me. Oh, I'm not the only person in the world who has lived many times, but there aren't many of us who have been regularly reincarnated. And if any of my old friends were alive in another shape or form, I'd know it. I'd *feel* it.'

Ken wished he could see the medium's expression. This woman sounded like a real nut. He glanced at Amanda, and then quickly looked away. He had to avoid making eye contact with her or they'd both start laughing out loud.

Cassandra turned to the boy sitting next to Ken. 'Would you like to introduce yourself?'

'I'm Stevie Fisher.' The boy sounded nervous. He was thin and fair-haired, and looked a couple of years younger than Ken.

'Who would you like to contact, Stevie?'

'My dad.'

'When did your father die?' the medium asked.

'A couple of months ago. It was a car accident.'

'And is there a particular reason you want to contact him?'

Stevie nodded. 'I have to ask him something.'

'Yes?' the medium prompted him.

The boy brushed a lock of hair out of his eyes. 'Well, a few days before my father had his accident, I was in a shop with him. And my dad bought a lottery ticket. I don't know why – he didn't usually buy lottery tickets. Maybe he just felt lucky . . .' His voice trailed off.

'Go on,' the veiled woman said.

Stevie sighed. 'The day the winning numbers were announced, he was at work. He called home, all excited, and told my mother he'd won! And the jack-pot was two million dollars!'

Ken gasped. He knew about the weekly lottery, of course, but he'd never bought a ticket. And he'd never known or met anyone who had actually won it.

Stevie continued. 'But . . . he was in an accident on the way home. He died right away. And we don't know where the ticket is.'

'Maybe it was in his pocket,' Ken suggested.

'No, we thought of that. But the police only found his wallet.'

'Maybe someone else found the ticket and took it,' Dahlia said.

Again Stevie shook his head. 'No one ever

claimed the prize. We think the ticket is somewhere in the house, but we've searched everywhere and we can't find it.'

'Oh, well,' Dahlia said. 'Who needs two million dollars anyway?'

'We do,' Stevie said simply. 'Well, we don't need *that* much, but we need money. You see, my father didn't have any life insurance. Or any savings. I've got two little sisters and one of them isn't even school age, so my mother has to stay at home and take care of her. When I get home I mind her, and Mom goes to clean other people's houses. But she doesn't make much money, and we can't pay the rent on our house. The landlord says we have one more month, and then he's throwing us out.'

It was a long speech for a young boy, and it couldn't have been an easy one for him to make. For a moment, everyone was silent.

Finally, the medium spoke. 'You want to ask your father where he put the lottery ticket.'

Stevie nodded. 'I have to help my family. I don't want us to end up homeless.'

Ken was overcome. What a burden for a kid to carry on his shoulders.

'Then we need to reach your father,' Cassandra said. 'And we have to make contact within a month. I suggest we get started.' She gazed around the table.

'Please join hands and close your eyes. The seance begins.'

Chapter Six

EVERYONE'S EYES WERE CLOSED – except Amanda's. She didn't want to miss a thing.

Ken had obeyed the medium's instructions, which was fortunate for Amanda, because he wouldn't be able to see how she was staring at him. He really was so good-looking. And even though he didn't play soccer any more, he still looked like an athlete. She'd been after him for ages, and now they could be on the verge of a real relationship! A happy little thrill rushed through her. Even the prospect of a hospital stay and an operation didn't upset her as much now.

The medium spoke.

'We have come together to seek advice from those who have left us behind,' she intoned.

Amanda envisioned herself sitting up in bed

wearing her new lacy pale blue nightgown, her hair pulled back with a matching headband, smiling as Ken walked into her room. Bearing armfuls of flowers, of course. Maybe a box of chocolates. She didn't mind giving up her tonsils at all if it meant getting a relationship with Ken started.

As for this seance thing, she wasn't sure what she thought about it. The medium looked spooky, but she spoke nicely to everyone. That Dahlia woman, with her crazy clothes and make-up, was seriously goofy. Margaret . . . she was just plain sad. And not just because her mother had recently died. She looked terrible, in a bulky grey jumper that was too big for her. It hung over a long, wrinkled, faded black skirt. You couldn't even tell what kind of figure she had. And that hair – had the woman ever been to a salon? OK, maybe not lately, because she was mourning her mother . . . but that hair looked like it had never been touched by profes-sional hands. And those glasses she wore were absolutely gross. Nobody wore tortoiseshell frames any more.

The medium was still talking. 'We know there is

a world beyond our own, a world of mystical mystery and energy which we can never understand. And in this spirit world, there is great wisdom.'

Amanda tuned out again. What about that kid, Stevie? She had serious doubts about him. He might look young and innocent, but that story of his was just too crazy to be true.

Cassandra continued, in a soft monotone. 'We seek you, oh spirits who dwell beyond our comprehension. We bid you come closer to accept our pleas.'

Yeah, whatever, Amanda thought. She was still more interested in scoping out Stevie. What was his deal? Why would he make up a story like that? She couldn't think of a reason. Unless, maybe, he was hoping someone somewhere had lost a winning lottery ticket, and some dead person would tell Cassandra where it was. It seemed like a far-fetched scheme though.

Cassandra's voice rose. 'I am being contacted! A spirit from the world beyond wishes to connect with one of our group.'

Dahlia let out a little squeal. 'Is he on a horse?'

'No . . . and it's not a "he", it's a female spirit.'

Amanda caught the flash of disappointment on Stevie's face.

'Maybe it's my former mother-in-law,' Dahlia mused. 'Is she wearing a hoop skirt? It was during the Civil War. I was a Yankee from up north married to a southern boy, and his mother just hated me. It would be just like her to start haunting me now.'

'No,' the medium said, and her voice was a little sharper this time. 'It's not your mother-in-law. Please, I must have quiet. We could frighten her away. She will not come closer and identify herself unless we remain silent.'

Silence reigned at the table. Amanda wondered if Cassandra was really making contact with a dead person. She wished she knew what Ken was thinking. She'd have to wait till they left before she found out if he believed the medium was for real or not.

'She is coming closer!' the medium exclaimed softly. 'She is speaking to me . . .' She gasped. 'It's your mother, Margaret.'

'Mama?' the woman murmured.

'Yes, yes, she is here, Margaret. What would you like to tell her?'

'I miss you, Mama . . . Oh, why did you leave me?'

Amanda could hear the pain in her voice. She couldn't imagine how she'd feel if her own mother died.

Cassandra spoke. 'She says it was not her choice to leave you, Margaret.'

'You were the only person I could trust, the only person I loved.' Now Margaret was weeping. 'I can't bear this! I want to be with you.'

Amanda drew in her breath. This was so hard to hear. The poor woman – she was so sad!

'Your mother says, don't think like that. You mustn't die – this is not your time. You must live, and keep her memory alive.'

'But I'm all alone,' Margaret wept. 'You were the only person who cared about me, the only one who loved me. I'm so lonely now . . .'

There was a lump in Amanda's throat, and for a moment she thought she was going to burst into tears herself. And she wasn't even thinking about how badly dressed Margaret was. This woman had absolutely nothing going for her. She was suffering, she was utterly despondent. Her words, her tears – they'd brought a cloud of sadness into the room and it was descending on Amanda . . . Wait – she recognized this feeling. She'd had it before.

Ohmigod, Ohmigod, oh no, oh no, this can't be happening, not here, not now . . . She closed her eyes and concentrated fiercely. I don't care about Margaret, she means nothing to me, I feel nothing for her . . .

But it was no use. She could feel it happening. And when she opened her eyes, she could feel a fringe tickling her forehead and she was looking through thick tortoiseshell frames. She was looking through someone else's eyes. Margaret's eyes.

Nobody else had noticed. Their eyes were still closed, but it wouldn't have mattered if they'd been watching her. This had happened before and no one had been aware, except her.

Actually, there *was* one other person whose eyes were open. The person who looked like Amanda.

Who wasn't even really a person, just some sort of automatic fake-Amanda, programmed to act like her. Flesh and blood, but more like a robot than a human being.

'Your mother has to go now, Margaret,' the medium said. 'But she'll come back another time to talk to you again. Do you have anything to say before she leaves?'

There was a silence. It took Amanda a few seconds before she realized *she* had to respond for Margaret.

'Uh . . . bye.'

'She is gone,' Cassandra said. 'And I'm afraid there are no other spirits waiting to speak with us tonight. But do not despair. This is just the beginning. The spirits have been called, and they will respond. We will meet again on Monday evening.'

Amanda-Margaret rose quickly. She had to let Ken know what had happened to her. But that woman Dahlia clamped a hand on her arm.

'You poor dear, I feel so sorry for you. Why don't we go out and have a nice cocktail together?'

'Sorry, no – I can't,' Amanda said, pulling free with

some effort. She turned – and saw Ken with Other-Amanda, walking out the door. She took off after them, and ran out of the apartment . . . only to see the lift doors closing behind them. Frantically, she looked for the stairs. She flew down the four flights, but when she arrived at the hallway she was greeted by an open lift, with no one inside.

She went outside, with absolutely no idea where she was going. Her heart – Margaret's heart – was pounding furiously, and she took deep breaths to keep her rising panic under control. She heard voices behind her and hurried around to the side of the apartment building, where no one would see her. She had to collect her thoughts, work out what she was going to do.

She found a bench and sat down. That was when she realized that Margaret's handbag was still slung across her chest. She opened it and found a wallet. Inside the wallet there was a driver's licence. In the dark the photo wasn't clear, but she could make out a name – Margaret Robinson – and an address. There were keys in the bag too. So Margaret probably came here in a car . . . but there were more than a dozen cars parked on either side of this street. How would she know which one was Margaret's?

And what did it matter even if she could identify Margaret's car? Amanda didn't know how to drive.

She explored the pockets in the wallet. Well, that was a relief – there had to be at least fifty dollars in it. She had an address, keys, and money for a taxi. So at least she could get home.

She walked down to the first major street and flagged down a taxi. Giving the driver the address she'd found, she leaned back in the seat and considered her situation. So, now she had become a depressed and badly dressed woman living a sad and lonely life. Why couldn't she ever snatch the body of someone *cool*?

At least Margaret didn't live in a dump. The taxi pulled up in front of a modern building in a decent part of town. Amanda paid the driver and got out. One of the keys unlocked the front door, and she found the name Robinson on one of the postboxes in the hall. Noting the apartment number, she took the lift up to the third floor.

In the seance, Margaret had talked about being so alone. That meant she probably didn't have flatmates. That was good — Amanda wouldn't have to start communicating like Margaret straight away. Another key opened the apartment door. Feeling along the wall, she located a light switch and pushed it.

She was pleasantly surprised by what she saw. She'd imagined Margaret living in a place that looked as depressing as she did. But this apartment was very nice. It wasn't a grand, fancy place, but it was modern, well-furnished, and even trendy. There were hanging plants, a colourful rug on the floor, pictures on the walls. A big framed poster from a rock concert hung over the sofa. Funny — Margaret hadn't seemed like the kind of person who went to rock concerts. There was a framed photograph on an end table, showing five good-looking people in their twenties on what looked like a tropical beach. Friends of Margaret's? But then why was she so lonely?

Amanda moved into what she thought would be a bedroom. She was right, and once again, it was a stylish room. There was a bright blue and white duvet on the big four-poster bed, big fluffy pillows, and a large white dressing table with a matching chest of drawers. A huge full-length mirror was on the wall, and there was a big walk-in wardrobe. *That* got Amanda's full attention. She went inside, switched on the light and gasped. Margaret had clothes, and lots of them. On a wall were shelves covered with shoes. Checking things out, Amanda could see that the clothes and shoes weren't the best brands. Most were from discount stores that sold cheaper versions of the hot new looks, but the things she found were a lot better looking than the awful baggy sweater and wrinkled skirt she had on now.

Why was Margaret wearing this? Just because she was in mourning for her mother? It seemed to Amanda that you didn't have to dress like an old bag lady just to show you were sad about your mother's death.

She wandered over to the mirror and examined herself. Taking off the glasses, she found her reflection disturbing. Not just because Margaret was so drab — it was something else. That pasty skin — it didn't look natural. She rubbed Margaret's cheek, and then looked at her hand. It was stained with white powdery stuff. Peering closer at her reflection, she saw a spot of normal-looking skin on the cheek.

Hurrying into the bathroom, she took a washcloth and scrubbed her face. More powder came off, and more real skin was visible. It wasn't just ordinary skin either. Margaret had a nice golden tan! Why had she covered it? Maybe she thought it would look wrong to have a tan so soon after her mother's death.

It wasn't just puzzlement that made Amanda scratch her head. It had been itching for a while now, and after scratching harder, she realized why. Margaret was wearing a wig.

This was getting weirder and weirder. When Amanda lifted the wig off, Margaret's own hair turned out to be a much nicer shade of light brown with some blonde streaks – the kind that must have been put in by a good hairdresser. The hair had been flattened down by the wig, but once Amanda poked at it with a comb for a while, she could see that Margaret had a cute layered bob. And when she took off the baggy skirt and sweater, she discovered that Margaret had a good figure too.

Rummaging in Margaret's chest of drawers, she found skinny jeans and a tight-fitting top. A box on top of the dressing table contained lots of make-up, all good brands. She applied eyeliner, mascara, a little blusher and a rose-pink lipstick. Then she stepped back from the mirror and examined herself again.

Margaret was cute! If she'd looked like this at the seance Amanda would never have felt so sorry for her, not even with her sad story. Well, OK, she might have felt a little sorry for her because her mother had died, but not so much that she'd do a body-snatch.

She went back into the living room and looked at the photo on the end table again. Now she recognized Margaret as one of the attractive young people on the beach. That was probably where she'd got her tan. She took the wallet out of Margaret's bag and examined the driver's licence again. She could see the photo clearly now, and Margaret looked pretty much like Amanda had just made her look. So Amanda hadn't given her a makeover – this was how Margaret normally dressed. Exploring further, she found a couple of credit cards in the wallet too.

It dawned on her that it might not be so awful being Margaret Robinson for a little while. She wouldn't mind living in this apartment. And she was twenty-five years old! She could go to clubs and hang out in places that would never let a fourteen-year-old in.

And there was something else – if she remained in this body up to Monday, robot-Amanda would have the operation in her place! Yes, there was a lot about this situation that could work to her advantage.

A phone rang. It sounded like a mobile, so she dived back into Margaret's handbag.

'Hello?'

'Hi, Margie, it's me.' The voice was a woman's.

Amanda tried to sound casual. 'Oh, hi. How are you?'

'Fine. Well, burning up, actually. It's ninety-nine degrees here, and our air conditioner's broken.'

Amanda didn't know what the temperature was outside, but she was very sure it wasn't anywhere near ninety-nine degrees. It had been cool when she left the seance.

'Where are you?' she asked.

The woman sounded amused. 'Where do you think I am? Miami, of course. You'll be coming down to visit next month, won't you?'

'Um, I guess. I'll try.'

'You *must* come,' the woman said. 'It's been too long. We'll send you money for a flight. Daddy and I want to see you. Wait, he wants to say hello.'

A man spoke. 'Margie, listen to your mother. We'll expect you in December.'

'OK. I have to go now. Bye.'

'Here, say goodbye to your mother.'

'Bye, Margie!' the woman chirped.

Amanda swallowed. 'Bye . . . Mom.'

They were disconnected. Amanda just stood there for a minute, still holding the phone. Daddy. *Mom.*

What was going on here?

CHAPTER SEVEN

*S*O HOW DID IT *go with Amanda?*

Ken yawned. It was Saturday morning, he was still in bed, and for once he didn't mind having a chat with his old friend.

I don't know. She was sort of weird.

How do you mean, weird?

Well, like, at first things were really good. I mean, we were kind of connecting, you know? We talked a lot on the way there. And during the seance I couldn't even look at her because I was afraid we'd start laughing. I thought things were going pretty well for us.

Cool.

But then things changed. After the seance, coming home, she barely spoke to me. I asked her if she wanted to get something to eat, but she said she wasn't hungry.

So I took her home. And she didn't invite me to come in.

Did you kiss her?

I didn't even get a chance. The second we arrived at her place, she went inside and closed the door. She didn't even say goodbye!

That's pretty weird. Maybe she's just not into you. Hey, what are you doing today?

I don't know. I haven't thought about it.

Why don't you go to the pool?

The indoor pool at the Community Centre? Nah, it's too crowded on Saturdays.

Oh, c'mon, you could use a good swim. Work out your frustrations over Amanda. And you'd be doing me a favour.

How's that?

Lucy goes to the pool every Saturday. It'll give you a chance to talk to her. Find out what's going on between her and Dowell.

Ken sighed. Well, if he was going to help Jack he'd have to talk to Lucy sooner or later, and he might as well get it over with. The pool was as good a place as any.

When he arrived, he saw that the pool wasn't as crowded as he'd expected. He didn't see Lucy around so he decided to make the most of it. He dived in.

The thing he liked best about swimming was that he could put his mind on automatic pilot and let his thoughts wander. And his thoughts went back to Amanda. He hoped *she* didn't go to the pool on Saturdays. Nah, the public swimming pool was probably beneath her.

She'd really been a major disappointment, he thought as he swam his lengths. He'd been feeling positive about her at the seance and when the seance was over he'd looked forward to discussing what they'd just observed, and comparing their reactions.

But Amanda had been totally uninterested in having any kind of conversation. When he tried to talk to her, she acted like the whole thing had been boring. She just kept shrugging her shoulders and saying, 'Whatever'. He'd asked her if she was worrying about her operation, and all she said was that she hoped she could get a manicure at the hospital! She was like a different person from the one he'd gone to the seance with. Maybe Jack was right, and she just wasn't into him. Maybe she'd decided his 'gift' really did make him a freak.

When he emerged from the pool, he saw that Lucy had arrived. She was setting down her bag beside a table and chairs, and she was alone. He ambled over to her.

'Hi.'

She looked up. 'Oh, hi, Ken. How's Jack?'

'Fine,' he murmured, hoping no one he knew could overhear their conversation.

She pulled out a chair for herself and one for Ken. 'Sit down.'

He did.

'I was just wondering, what's it like, talking to a dead person?'

Ken couldn't meet her eyes. 'It's hard to describe.'

'Did you contact more dead people at the seance?' she asked.

'Some people did. Not me.'

'Do you ever talk to dead people besides Jack? Anyone famous?'

'No, nobody famous. Listen, Lucy, I really don't like talking about this, OK?'

She nodded. 'I can understand that. Because most people aren't as open-minded as I am. They'd think you were nuts.'

He couldn't argue with that. Just then, Lucy's handbag started to beep.

'Ooh, I've got a text message,' she said. She fumbled in her bag and pulled out her phone. She punched some buttons and looked at the screen. 'Yay!' she exclaimed.

'Good news?' Ken enquired politely.

'Simon Dowell wants to know if I'll go to the basketball game with him on Tuesday evening.'

'Oh.' He scratched his head. 'Are you going to go?'

'Sure. Why not?'

'Um, well . . . you know, Simon has a reputation. I've heard he's kind of a player, if you know what I mean. Do you really like him?'

Lucy shrugged. 'He's OK. But if you don't think I should go out with him, I won't.'

He wished he could tell her it was *Jack* who was concerned, not him. 'Well, I can't tell you what to do. I just wanted to warn you.'

'Thank you, Ken. Listen . . . what are you doing later?'

'Later?'

'Mm. Like, tonight.'

'Tonight?' he repeated stupidly.

'I thought maybe you'd like to come over to my place.' She lowered her eyes demurely. 'My parents are going out.'

Ken swallowed. 'Uh, thanks, but, no, um, I have to do something. See ya, Lucy.' He jumped up and hurried to the boys' locker room. Once he was safe in all-male territory, he leaned against the wall and let out the breath he'd been holding. Oh, *great*. She thought he was interested in her – and *not* in a big brother way. What had Jack got him into? Man, if his best friend wasn't already dead, Ken would have killed him.

Maybe Jack heard his thoughts, because he didn't try to contact Ken the rest of the weekend, and Ken could think about more important subjects. Like the next seance on Monday.

He'd decided he was definitely going back. That Cassandra, the medium – Ken didn't have any experience with mediums, but she seemed like the real thing. Her voice, when she related the messages from Margaret's mother, sounded sincere to him. Like she was really listening to another voice, and like she really cared.

That poor Margaret! He hoped the medium would be able to help her. Maybe if she knew her mother was OK, in heaven or whatever, she'd feel better and be able to get on with her life. The older woman, Dahlia – she seemed a little nuts, but it was possible she actually had experienced other lives. Lots of intelligent people believed in reincarnation.

But the one who had really touched him was Stevie. The boy really cared about his family, and he was desperate to help them.

Ken was dying to talk about this, to share the experience. But he couldn't tell his friends – they'd just laugh. And how could he explain his own interest without revealing his gift? Lucy knew about it, but he was afraid to talk to her about anything. She'd only think he was coming on to her. So for once he was really looking forward to the gifted class. His classmates were the only people he could tell.

He arrived early at class that Monday. Emily was the only other student already there.

'I bought a Get Well Soon card for Amanda,' she told Ken. 'Will you sign it?'

Ken grimaced. Of course he'd have to sign it – it would be childish and mean to refuse. And it wasn't as if he wanted her to die, or suffer terribly. But what would he write?

Emily had already contributed her message. 'Hi, Amanda, we miss you!!! Get well quickly!!! Love, Emily.'

After thinking a moment, he scrawled, 'I hope you feel better soon. Best wishes, Ken Preston.' It was the kind of thing you'd write on a card that was going to someone you barely knew. But that was how he felt about her now.

He sat at his desk and waited impatiently for the others to arrive. Emily made each of them sign the card, and when Madame arrived she had to sign it too.

As soon as the bell rang, his hand flew up. So did Tracey's. Madame called on her first.

'Madame, could we take up a collection to send Amanda some flowers?'

'That's a nice idea, Tracey,' Madame said.

Charles didn't think so. 'Her family's rich. They can afford to buy her plenty of flowers.'

Madame frowned. 'That's not the point, Charles. We want Amanda to know we're thinking about her.'

Martin raised his hand. '*I'm* not thinking about her.'

Jenna turned to him. 'Just fake it, Martin. It's the right thing to do.'

'I think she likes roses,' Tracey said. 'Yellow ones would be nice.'

'Roses are really expensive,' Emily said. 'I don't know if we'll be able to collect that much money. Are tulips in season now?'

Ken slumped in his seat. Personally, he felt like agreeing with Charles and Martin. But mainly he wanted this discussion of flowers to end so he could bring up his news.

Finally the money was collected and Emily said she'd go to the florist and see what kind of flowers they could buy. The second she finished speaking, Ken put his hand up, and Madame nodded to him.

'There's something I want to tell the class about,' he said. 'Last Friday night I went to a seance.'

'What's a seance?' Martin asked.

Madame answered for Ken. 'It's a ritual where people try to contact friends and family who have passed on.' She frowned. 'What were you doing there, Ken?'

'I just thought it would be interesting,' he said. 'To meet people who do what I do.'

Now Madame looked seriously concerned. 'Did you participate in the seance, Ken? Did you let people know about your gift?'

'No, no, nothing like that,' he assured her. 'I was just listening. Anyway, there was this kid—'

He was interrupted before he could get any further. 'Are you nuts?' Jenna asked. 'Those things are scams.'

'You don't know if that's true,' he declared. 'Hey, if *I* can talk to the dead, there must be other people who can do it.'

But Madame was shaking her head. 'That's not necessarily true, Ken. Your gift may be unique.'

'I don't think so,' Ken argued. 'This medium,

Cassandra, she wants to help people. She doesn't even charge money for coming to the seance.'

Madame didn't look convinced. 'I'm sorry, Ken, but I don't think it's a good idea for you to attend meetings like that. You'll be urged to join in. You may feel compelled to share your gift.'

Ken scowled. 'I can control myself, Madame.'

'That's not true,' Jenna interjected. 'You're always saying how you can't control your gift.'

Ken glared at her. 'I meant, I know how to keep my mouth shut.'

'I'm sure you do,' Madame said smoothly. 'But Ken, you'll encounter temptations. Perhaps a participant in the seance will be desperate to contact a deceased loved one and you'll actually receive a message from that person who's passed on. You'll want to relay the message.'

She had a point, and Ken found it extremely annoying. It was as if she didn't trust him to behave properly. And his classmates weren't sympathetic either.

'Do you understand what we're saying, Ken?' Madame asked.

He shrugged. 'Whatever.'

But that evening he told his parents he was going to the library. Instead he went back to Cassandra's apartment.

He got there early, but he wasn't the first to arrive. Dahlia was already there, having an intense conversation with Cassandra.

'I knew Cleopatra very well, you see. I was one of her handmaidens. And I told her over and over again, "Cleo, Mark Antony is worth a dozen Caesars." But would she ever listen to me? That woman had a mind of her own. She could be so stubborn.'

He really didn't want to get caught up in this conversation, and he was relieved when Stevie arrived next.

'Hey, how's it going?' he asked the younger boy.

Stevie didn't look any more cheerful than he'd looked at the last seance.

'OK, I guess,' he said. 'Mom took Dad's old clothes to a second-hand shop and sold them. We didn't get much though.' He smiled sadly. 'It's not like he wore designer clothes.'

Ken nodded sympathetically, and Stevie continued.

'I've been trying to get a job delivering newspapers, but you have to be twelve and I'm only eleven.' He looked at Ken hopefully. 'Do you know anyone who would hire me? I'm very mature for my age. I could run errands, mow lawns, carry groceries . . .'

'I'll ask my mother,' Ken promised him. 'Listen, I get a pretty decent allowance. I could give you a few bucks . . .'

Stevie shook his head violently. 'I won't take charity,' he stated firmly. Ken could see that he was trying to look older than his eleven years. It made Ken hurt inside. He wished the medium would pay more attention to the boy and less to the lady with the past lives. Dahlia just wanted to say hi to old friends but Stevie was in serious need of help.

Another woman walked in, and it took Ken a minute to realize she was Margaret. She looked completely different tonight. Her hair was shorter, she wore jeans, and she was − well, kind of pretty! He was amazed. Had that brief message from her mother completely changed her life?

Cassandra seemed very surprised to see her too.

She ushered them all to the table, but she kept looking at Margaret with a puzzled expression.

They joined hands and the medium began. 'Oh spirits, hear our fervent plea. We are in great need of your presence. Please speak with us tonight.'

The group was silent, and Ken concentrated very hard. Maybe something would happen for Stevie tonight.

'A spirit is approaching,' the medium said. 'I am getting a message.'

Ken held his breath. Oh please, he thought, let it be Stevie's father.

After a moment she added, 'It's a man,' and his heart leapt. Come on, Mr Fisher, Stevie needs you.

Then Cassandra said, 'He's carrying red roses,' and Dahlia let out a squeal.

'It's Vladimir!' she cried out. 'He always brought me red roses.'

Ken opened his eyes. 'Who's Vladimir?'

'My lover, in Russia,' Dahlia said. 'Before the Revolution. Does he have a message for me?'

'Yes,' Cassandra said. 'He wants you to know he waits for you in eternity.'

'Oh, how lovely,' Dahlia said happily. 'I have such wonderful memories of my time with Vladimir. I'm so happy to know he still thinks of me.'

Ken couldn't help rolling his eyes, and then he realized Margaret was looking straight at him. And she was smiling! He was so surprised, he couldn't even smile back at her. He closed his eyes.

The medium had more words from Vladimir for Dahlia — mushy stuff that almost made Ken blush. Finally Vladimir made an exit, and Cassandra was available to hear from another spirit.

'Margaret, your mother is here.'

'Oh, yeah?'

'She wants to know if you've been taking your vitamins.'

'Uh, sure.'

'She wants you to know she's watching you, Margaret.'

'OK.'

'And thinking about you.'

'Great,' Margaret said. 'Tell her I'm thinking about her too.'

Ken opened his eyes again. There was no sign

of a tear on Margaret's face. He noticed that, above the veils, the medium's eyes were open too. Ken didn't blame her. This was a completely different Margaret from the one they'd seen the previous Friday.

'Well,' Cassandra said finally, 'your mother is very pleased to see you're feeling better. She wants to say goodbye now.'

'Bye, Mom,' Margaret said.

The medium noticed that Ken's eyes were open, and she frowned. Obediently, he closed them.

'Someone else is coming,' Cassandra said. 'I think it may be Cleopatra, Dahlia.'

Ken uttered a silent groan. Where was Stevie's father? Didn't the man realize how desperately Stevie needed to talk to him?

He made a decision. As soon as the seance was over he was going to have a private conversation with the medium. Despite Madame's warning, he was going to tell her about his gift.

Because together, if they joined forces, they just might be able to help Stevie.

Hey, man, what's up?

Jack, not now! I'm in the middle of a seance. I'm trying to concentrate!

But did you talk to Lucy? Did you tell her not to go out with Simon?

Yeah, I told her.

Thanks, pal. Look, could you do something else for me? You've still got my iPod, right? I left it at your place a couple of days before I died, remember?

I think so. Why?

Could you give it to Lucy for me? And tell her it's from me?

OK, OK. Jack, listen, I gotta go. I really want to concentrate on this seance.

Sure, man. See ya.

Ken opened his eyes for a minute, and realized that Cassandra's eyes were open too. And she was looking straight at him. Maybe she'd sensed he hadn't been paying attention. Obediently, he closed his eyes and thought about Stevie's father.

But Cleopatra was the last dead person to speak to them that night.

CHAPTER EIGHT

AMANDA WAS RELIEVED WHEN the medium turned her attention to Dahlia. It wasn't easy, pretending to talk to Margaret's dead mother. Especially when she knew Margaret's mother wasn't dead at all.

What was Margaret up to anyway? She'd been in Margaret's body for almost three days now, and she was no closer to an answer. But she wasn't letting the question drive her crazy. She was having too much fun for that.

Bored with the conversation between Dahlia and Cleopatra, she closed her eyes and let her mind drift back, to remember and relive the very interesting weekend she'd just enjoyed . . .

Once she recovered from the shock of learning that Margaret wasn't a drab, depressed woman with a dead mother, she explored the apartment to learn who she really was. Unfortunately, Margaret didn't keep a diary – at least, Amanda couldn't find one. There were photos – more of Margaret on the tropical beach, plus pictures of her at what looked like a party. She didn't see any pictures of her alone with a guy, so she assumed Margaret didn't have a current boyfriend. She was glad – it might be hard to fool a boyfriend into believing she was really Margaret. In fact, she decided it would be best to spend the next few days on her own, and try not to encounter any of Margaret's close friends. After seeing the credit cards in the wallet, she knew she could have a very nice time all by herself.

After a good night's sleep in Margaret's comfy bed, Amanda woke feeling refreshed and ready to begin her new life as a twenty-five-year-old adult. Having watched a great many television series about young single women, she had some good ideas as to how she could spend the weekend.

From Margaret's closet, she selected leggings, a tunic top and a pair of stilettos. It was the very first time she'd worn heels this high, and she felt positively glamorous. Once outside, she walked to the closest bus stop. She would have preferred to take a taxi, but she'd already made a dent in Margaret's cash resources. There was a cash card in the wallet, but she didn't know Margaret's PIN code, so she would have to be careful with the money. It was a good thing she had the two credit cards.

A *very* good thing. Because her first stop was the Mall.

There were many shops she liked, but Unique Boutique was her favourite. It had the trendiest clothes in town, and a notice in the window assured her that Margaret's credit cards would be accepted. She spent a few minutes just looking at the window displays, revelling in the knowledge she could have anything she wanted.

Did Margaret ever go to this store? she wondered. She doubted it – she hadn't seen anything in her closet with the labels carried here. Unique Boutique was probably too expensive for Margaret. But that was what credit cards were for – to buy things you couldn't afford, right?

It was funny – people thought Amanda's family was rich and that she could have anything she wanted. This wasn't exactly true. Maybe her parents *were* rich, but they didn't spend all their money on her. And contrary to popular opinion, she wasn't spoiled – at least, *she* didn't consider herself spoiled. Her parents didn't give her everything she wanted, like her own credit cards. She had to ask for stuff, and sometimes they said no. And she didn't have many items from Unique Boutique.

But there was no one to say no to her today. She didn't have to get anyone's permission to buy anything. She could have it all.

Like that unbelievably cute slinky red party dress with the wide black belt . . . She could just hear her mother saying, 'Amanda, you do not need another party dress.' Amanda smiled happily and went into the store. She found the dress in her size, didn't even look at the price tag, and headed to the dressing room.

There, she encountered an unusual problem. The dress didn't fit. She couldn't even do the zip up. What was going on here? She didn't think she'd gained any weight . . .

Then it hit her and she groaned. Of course the

dress wouldn't fit her. She'd chosen the size that Amanda Beeson wore. Margaret was taller, wider in the hips and much bigger on top.

Well, it wasn't such a terrible problem. All she had to do was change back into her clothes, return to the rack and pick out some larger sizes to take back to the dressing room to try on. But then something else occurred to her. Amanda Beeson wouldn't be emerging from this spending spree with a new wardrobe, Margaret Robinson would.

It wasn't like Amanda was going to be Margaret forever. She didn't know how long she'd be in this body – she'd been in Tracey for two whole weeks, after all – but now, after three big bodysnatching experiences, she was pretty sure she'd be able to get back into herself when she wanted to get out of Margaret. All it seemed to take was a little physical shake-up. Just last month, a slip on a freshly waxed floor had got her out of Sarah. She planned to stay in Margaret until the other-Amanda got out of the hospital and recovered, and Margaret's life stopped being interesting.

But the realization that Margaret would be

keeping the fabulous clothes she bought had taken much of the joy out of her plans for the day. Maybe she could buy the clothes in her own size and figure out a way to take them with her when she returned to her own body. But that would be sort of like stealing . . .

In the end, she half-heartedly bought the slinky dress and a cashmere sweater. After another hour of wandering around the Mall, her feet hurt and she was forced to buy a pair of sneakers in Margaret's size. Stilettos were not meant for shopping, she decided.

The day improved considerably when she decided to indulge in expensive treats that she could enjoy while she was in Margaret's body. She went to an expensive salon and got a few more blonde streaks added to brighten Margaret's hair. She treated herself to lunch at a chic café, and then went to her mother's favourite day spa for a facial, a massage and a manicure. From there she went to the cosmetic counter at a major department store and had a complete makeover.

Then it was happy hour – at least according to

those single-girl TV shows she watched. Changing into the slinky dress, she put the stilettos back on and went to a bar she'd read about in a magazine. The article said it was the hippest place in town.

She liked the look of the bar – all black and silver and glass. It was elegant and stylish. The customers looked nice too, well-dressed and good-looking. There were little pedestal tables with high stools alongside them, and behind the bar, a very handsome man was mixing drinks.

Amanda went to the bar and sat on a stool. The bartender smiled at her and asked, 'What can I get you?'

She hadn't even considered what she'd drink. She'd look like an idiot if she ordered a Coke or orange juice or something like that in this kind of place. They might not even have drinks like that here.

Back home, her parents sometimes had a glass of wine with dinner, and her father had let her taste his wine a couple of times. She'd never really liked the taste – sort of like grape juice, but sour. Maybe now that she was in an adult's body she might like it.

'I'd like a glass of wine, please,' she said.

'Sure, what kind? A white wine? We've got a fruity Chardonnay, and a nice crisp Chablis. Or a Pinot Grigio, if you like that. It's very dry.'

Amanda just stared at him blankly.

'Would you prefer a red?' he asked. 'We have an excellent Merlot, and a hearty Burgundy.'

This was way too complicated. Amanda thought frantically. What did her father order in restaurants, before the meal?

'Um, I changed my mind. I'd like a Martini, please. Very dry.'

'Coming up,' the bartender said.

Amanda looked around. A man sitting alone at one of the high tables caught her eye. To her surprise, he grinned and winked at her. It made her distinctly uncomfortable. He was *old* – at least thirty. What was he doing, winking at a fourteen-year-old?

He doesn't know you're fourteen years old, she reminded herself. Quickly, she looked away. The bartender set a frosted glass with a long stem in front of her.

'One very dry Martini,' he announced. 'I threw in two olives. No extra charge.' Then *he* winked at her. All this winking was giving her the creeps. And she hated olives. When the bartender wasn't looking, she fished them out with her fingers. Then she held the drink to her lips and took a tentative sip.

It was *disgusting*. How did adults drink these things? It was all she could do not to gag.

Suddenly, she realized that the man who had winked at her earlier had come to the bar. There were several empty places, but he took the stool right next to her.

'Hi,' he said. 'Good to see you again.'

Oh no! It was somebody who knew Margaret. She should never have gone to a bar so near Margaret's apartment.

'Um, nice to see you too,' she murmured.

His eyebrows went up and he seemed pleased. 'Yeah? The way you blew me off last time, I didn't think you'd be so happy to see me.'

He whistled to the bartender and indicated Amanda's Martini. 'I'll have one of these,' he said. 'And put them both on my tab.'

Amanda's brow furrowed. 'You don't have to pay for my drink. I've got my own money.'

'My treat,' the man said. 'Now, let's get to know each other.'

Amanda fumbled in Margaret's bag, and took out what she hoped would be a large enough banknote.

'No, thank you,' she said quickly, putting it on the bar. 'I have to go.'

'You just got here!' The man's protests rang in her ears as she fled the bar. OK, maybe she wasn't ready for this kind of adult life.

But she still had the credit cards, and she'd found another card in Margaret's wallet – a video-club membership. She could still be an adult, in a different way. She used the credit card to buy food she normally never ate – fried chicken wings, French fries and sugar-packed soft drinks. Microwave popcorn with butter. And real ice cream, not that reduced-fat stuff they always had at home. For once in her life she didn't have to worry about gaining weight – these calories weren't going into *her* body!

At the video club she picked up movies that she

wouldn't have been allowed to see in a cinema. Not dirty stuff – just sophisticated films that were 'restricted to over-eighteens'. She brought her goodies back to Margaret's apartment and had a very enjoyable evening all by herself.

She told herself that on Sunday she'd do more 'adult' things, like go to a really fancy restaurant. Get a pedicure, or maybe have her legs waxed. Find a club where she could dance.

In the end, she spent all of Sunday doing what she did on Saturday night – eating junk food and watching movies. And totally enjoying herself. This was the kind of adult life she could handle.

On Monday morning she learned what Margaret did for a living. The phone woke her at seven a.m.

'Miss Robinson, this is Eastside Elementary School. We have a teacher who just called in sick. Could you substitute today?'

Amanda wasn't even tempted. 'Oh, I'm very sorry, but I'm sick myself. I'm about to have my tonsils out.'

She didn't even have to lie! Because right now, at the hospital across town, someone who looked like

Amanda Beeson — who *was* Amanda Beeson, physically at least — was being put to sleep before her operation.

Yes, it was a very pleasant weekend. But now she had to return to the present, and she looked at Ken across the table. His eyes were shut tightly, and he was gripping the hand of the young boy, Stevie.

'I can't seem to reach your father, Stevie,' the medium said, 'but I can feel him getting closer. We'll try again tomorrow.'

Ken opened his eyes. He glanced at Margaret, but his eyes didn't linger. *He doesn't have a clue*, Amanda marvelled. Wait till he hears this is *me!*

Once again, she didn't get the opportunity to tell him. When they rose from the table, Cassandra spoke to her.

'I must have a word with you, Margaret,' she said. 'Could you stay back for a minute?'

'OK,' Amanda said. 'I just need to—' but by then, Ken was already out of the apartment. Stevie was gone too.

Cassandra waited until Dahlia had left and then

she turned to Amanda. Her tone changed dramatically.

'What do you think you're doing?' she asked
shrilly. 'What's the matter with you?'

Amanda was startled. 'Huh?'

'Look at you! Nobody's going to believe you're
a grieving daughter! And you didn't behave today
the way we practised. Do you want to blow this
whole thing?'

'What do you mean?'

'I brought you in on this to make it look like a
real seance. You're supposed to be looking for your
dead mother and I'm pretending to talk to her for
you. You were fine last week – why are you screw-
ing up tonight?'

As she spoke, Cassandra tugged at the scarves that
veiled her face.

'I – I don't know . . .' Amanda sputtered, but she
didn't finish the sentence. She was suddenly speechless.

Because the last scarf had come off, releasing long,
thick blonde hair, and Amanda recognized the face
that had been hidden. The last time she'd seen that

face, its owner had been hypnotizing Emily in an effort to learn the next week's winning lottery numbers.

Cassandra the medium was Serena Hancock, the student teacher.

Chapter Nine

K EN HAD WANTED TO stay behind and talk to the medium, but Stevie looked so upset when he ran out that Ken had to go after him. On the street in front of the medium's building, he could see disappointment written all over the younger boy's face.

'Are you OK?' Ken asked.

'Yeah . . . well, no, not really. I thought she would have made contact with my father by now.'

'It's not that easy,' Ken said. 'Sometimes the spirits of dead people are totally open to communicating. You don't even have to look for them – they're there. Others are harder to find. Your father might not even be aware that he can get a message to you.'

Stevie looked at him curiously. 'How do you know so much about it?'

Ken couldn't meet his eyes. 'I've read a lot.'

Stevie stared at the ground. 'My youngest sister, Dena, she keeps getting these rashes. My mother thinks she might be allergic to something, and she wants to take her to a doctor for tests. Only we can't afford it. We don't have any medical insurance. And my other sister, Cindy . . . she's growing so fast, and now she's complaining her shoes are too tight. Only there's no money to buy her a new pair.'

Ken could see he was close to tears. 'Listen . . . you know the public library, on Slater Street?'

'Sure.'

'Well, I need a bunch of books for − for an English assignment,' Ken said. 'And I don't have time to go there. If you could go for me, and check out the books, I'd pay you for your time.'

Stevie gazed up at him. 'Really?'

'Yeah. Here, I'll give you a list.' Ken dived into his backpack. He didn't really have an assignment, but his English teacher had given everyone in the class a list of 'suggested reading' − not required − which meant nobody was going to read the books. But Stevie wouldn't know that. He handed the list to the boy.

'If you could get me, like, five of these and bring them to the seance tomorrow night, I could give you forty dollars.' He'd been stashing portions of his allowance every week for the past month, trying to save up for an iPhone. There had to be at least forty dollars in his desk drawer. 'Maybe more,' he added.

'Just to go to the library and check out books?' Stevie asked.

'Yeah. You'd be doing me a big favour. Like I said, I don't have the time. It's worth the money to me.'

Stevie's eyes were shining. 'Hey, thanks! See you tomorrow.'

Ken watched as he took off. Forty dollars, maybe fifty. That wouldn't pay for new shoes *and* a visit to the doctor. And it wasn't like Ken could provide money like that on a regular basis. Stevie and his family needed more. They needed that lottery ticket.

He was about to climb into bed that night when he remembered Jack's latest request. Opening the drawer of his desk, he poked around through the junk he stashed in there and finally found the iPod Jack had left behind. So he'd have to talk to Lucy again. At least this time he could make it clear that he was only doing this for Jack and she'd realize that Ken wasn't interested in her that way.

He went to sleep thinking about Stevie, and he was still thinking about him the next morning. By the end of the afternoon, when he entered the gifted class, he'd made a decision.

He wanted to talk about it, but he didn't get the opportunity right away. Emily was practically bursting with news.

'Tracey and I went to see Amanda at the hospital yesterday evening,' she told Madame and the class.

'How is she feeling?' Madame asked.

'The girl we saw is feeling OK,' Emily said, 'but it wasn't Amanda.'

'It was that fake-Amanda who takes over when the real Amanda is in someone else's body,' Tracey reported.

'Are you sure?' Madame asked.

Emily nodded vigorously. 'She had that blank expression, like there weren't any thoughts in her head. And she kept looking in a mirror and putting on lipgloss.'

'And filing her nails,' Tracey added.

'Sounds exactly like the real Amanda to me,' Jenna commented.

'Nah, I could see the difference,' Tracey said. 'I had the real one in me, remember? I can't explain it, but I could feel that it wasn't really her.'

'Does she know where the real Amanda is?' Sarah asked.

Tracey shook her head. 'No. I even tried asking her, but she just looked at me like I was speaking a foreign language. It was definitely the robot-Amanda or the other-Amanda – whatever you want to call her.'

Jenna snorted. 'That is *so* Amanda.'

'What do you mean, Jenna?' Madame asked.

'She'll do anything to get out of doing something she doesn't want to do. She does a bodysnatch so she won't have to go through the operation. She makes the other-Amanda have it instead.'

Ken agreed. 'Yeah, she's pretty selfish.'

Madame smiled slightly. 'Oh, I don't know if what she did was so terrible. Whatever takes over Amanda's body when she's not there – it's not a real person.

It's like an impression of Amanda. I don't believe it has any feelings.'

Jenna shrugged. 'OK, maybe the fake Amanda doesn't care if she has an operation. I don't think the real Amanda cares whether fake Amanda feels it or not, as long as *she* doesn't have to suffer.'

'I think,' Madame said slowly, 'that you're being a little hard on her, Jenna. But there's something else about this situation that I find interesting. Sarah, do you know what I mean?'

'Yes,' Sarah said. 'It's getting easier for Amanda to snatch bodies. Last month she took over my body because she was afraid she'd be kidnapped. But when she took over Tracey, it wasn't like that.'

Tracey nodded. 'She didn't want to be me but she felt sorry for me, so the bodysnatch just happened. Why would she feel sorry for Sarah? She just wanted to get out of her own body so she picked Sarah's.'

'But we don't know that for sure,' Madame pointed out. 'The only person who knows is Amanda. Ken, do you have an opinion about this?'

'No,' Ken said quickly. As far as he knew the others weren't aware that Amanda had taken over his body for a while, and he wanted to keep it that way. But in the back of his mind he'd always wondered – why had Amanda done that? Had she felt sorry for *him*?

'What does it matter anyway?' he asked.

Madame replied, 'It matters because we need to be aware of what we can and cannot do, so that we can rely on each other in the future.'

Ken grimaced. She was going to start talking about the dangers they faced again. And he had something more important to tell them.

'I've found a way I could use my gift to help someone,' he announced.

'How's that, Ken?' Madame asked.

He told them about Stevie, his dead father, the missing lottery ticket, and the plight of Stevie's family. 'I'm thinking . . . if I work with the medium, if we put our heads together, maybe we can reach Stevie's father and find out where the lottery ticket is.'

Madame frowned. 'Ken, we've talked about this before and I thought I'd made myself clear. You cannot tell anyone about your gift.'

'But why not? OK, I can understand why most of you have to keep your gifts secret, but bad guys have never been interested in me! Nobody's tried to get me to help rob a bank or anything like that. My gift doesn't have any value for criminals. Why can't I use it to help someone?'

'What about the rest of us?' Charles protested. 'If you tell the world about what you can do, it could lead people to this class. We could all be in danger.'

'Charles is right, Ken,' Madame declared. 'Revealing your gift can have serious consequences. If you can help Stevie without giving anything away, that's all right. But you can't tell Stevie *or* this medium what you can do.'

Ken slumped in his seat. He wasn't going to continue arguing this. If he could help Stevie on his own he would do it, no matter what Madame said. Would he be putting the whole class at risk? Maybe Madame was exaggerating.

But what did it matter anyway? He had no idea how to contact Stevie's father. He'd never contacted *anyone*. They came to him.

That appeared to be the case with live people too.

He'd completely forgotten about Lucy and Jack and the iPod, but when he left the gifted class, he found her waiting for him outside.

'I always wondered what goes on in that class,' she said. 'Do all of you talk to dead people?'

'No. Look, I've got something for you.'

She beamed. 'Really?'

He reached in his backpack and pulled out the iPod. 'It's from Jack. He told me to give it to you.'

'Oh. Well, tell him thank you.'

'Sure. I'll see you around.'

'Ken!'

'What?'

'I did what you told me to do.'

'What are you talking about?' he asked.

'I told Simon I didn't want to go out with him.'

'Oh. OK, good. I'm sure you'll find someone else to hang out with.'

She smiled coyly. 'I think I already have. Can we go to the basketball game tonight?'

Damn. 'Uh, gee, I can't go to the game, Lucy, I've got plans tonight. Bye.'

At least he didn't have to lie this time. There was no way he was going to miss the evening's seance.

When he arrived that evening Stevie was already there, and he presented Ken with a stack of books he'd checked out from the public library. Ken handed over forty-seven dollars, all the money he'd found in his dresser drawer. Stevie was thrilled.

'You know, Ken, I can do stuff like this for you every day,' he said eagerly.

Ken forced a smile, and nodded. 'Yeah, we'll see.' He could always make up errands to run. But where would he find the money to pay Stevie for them?

Crazy Dahlia was there, and Margaret. Ken absent-mindedly noticed that she didn't look quite as good as she had the day before. Not as bad as she'd looked the first time he saw her though. Her hair was kind of messy, and she had on those big brown glasses again. But she wasn't as pasty-pale.

Just as Cassandra called them to the table, there was a knock on the door.

'Well, it seems we have another participant tonight,' the medium said.

'I'll get the door,' Dahlia offered.

Ken, Cassandra and the others took their seats at the table. A moment later, Dahlia returned with the new person. Ken choked.

'Jenna!'

'Hi, Ken,' Jenna said in an artificially bright voice. She turned to the others. 'Ken is in my class at school. He was telling us about the seance, and it sounded so interesting, I just had to come.'

She must have followed him, Ken realized. And he didn't believe a word she'd just said. Jenna was not the kind of person who would believe in mediums and seances.

He couldn't see Cassandra's veiled face, but he could tell by her tone that she wasn't thrilled with this new addition to their group.

'My dear, a seance isn't for everyone. Do you have an open mind? Are you willing to connect with the spirit world? Will you be able to receive the spirits?'

'Actually, I was thinking I'd just watch this time,' Jenna said.

The medium shook her head. 'I'm afraid that's not possible. You can't simply observe a seance. Your mere presence could ruin the event. You could distract and interrupt the mood and frighten off any spirit who wishes to address someone.'

'Then I'll join the group and participate in the seance,' Jenna said.

'No, I cannot allow that,' Cassandra declared. 'I'm sorry, my dear, but I can feel that you are a non-believer. Please leave now.'

When Jenna didn't move, the medium did. She came around the table and faced Jenna.

'This is my apartment, my home. If you do not leave, I will call the police.'

Jenna gave up and went to the door. Cassandra waited until she was out of the apartment before returning to the table and beginning.

'Join us, spirits, in our quest to find answers . . .'

Thank goodness there was nothing for Dahlia that evening, but Margaret's mother returned.

'Your mother wants to know how you're feeling, Margaret.'

'I'm sad,' Margaret said. 'I miss you very much, Mama. I think about you all the time.'

It was pretty much the same thing she'd said last Friday, but Ken thought there was something different this time. Maybe it was her tone – she didn't sound like she was going to burst into tears. In fact her voice was almost wooden, like she'd memorized and rehearsed these lines.

'Your mother wants you to stay busy, Margaret,' the medium told her. 'That's the only way to get over your grief. She suggests that you find an interesting club to join. Birdwatching, perhaps.'

'Birdwatching?' Margaret exclaimed. 'Ick! Are you for real?'

Cassandra's voice was steely. 'This is your mother addressing you, Margaret.'

'Oh, right,' Margaret said. 'Sorry, Mom, I'll think about it.'

'Your mother's leaving us now, Margaret.'

'Don't leave, Mama!' Margaret cried out. 'Stay here, please. I'm begging you, don't go away, I'm so lonely and sad, I need you . . .'

Cassandra almost sounded impatient. 'She can't stay, Margaret. She'll be back tomorrow. Now let's try to call another spirit to us. Let us all be very quiet and concentrate very hard.'

Ken began a silent chant. *Mr Fisher, Mr Fisher, Mr*

Fisher, Mr Fisher . . .

'A spirit approaches,' Cassandra intoned. 'It is a man. He is calling a name. I'm having difficulty hearing him . . . Oh spirit, please, speak louder . . . Mr Fisher, is that you?'

'Dad?' Stevie cried out.

'Shh,' the medium murmured. 'Again, spirit, again, who do you wish to contact?' She drew in her breath. 'Your son? Your son . . . Stevie?'

Holding Stevie's hand, Ken could feel the boy's grip tighten.

'Do you have something you want to say to Stevie? Do you have a message for him?'

Ken couldn't breathe. Or maybe he was just feeling the tension in the boy sitting next to him.

'What is the message? Oh spirit, I cannot hear you! Your voice . . . it's too faint! Repeat! Repeat!'

And then Cassandra sighed. 'He's gone.'

'Oh, no!' Stevie cried out. 'Dad, come back!'

'I'm sorry, Stevie. It wasn't a good connection. But don't despair! We've made contact. He'll come back. Maybe I'm just not strong enough. If only there was another medium here, someone else who is also sensitive to the spirit world. Perhaps together we could forge a pathway.'

That was all Ken needed to hear. 'Can I talk to you privately, Cassandra?'

'Of course, Ken,' the medium said. To the others, she said, 'The seance is over. We will meet again at the same time tomorrow evening.'

Dahlia and Stevie went to the hallway and Dahlia opened the door. Jenna practically fell in, as if she'd been leaning against it.

'What are you doing here?' Cassandra demanded to know. 'I told you to leave!'

'I was waiting for Ken,' Jenna said. 'I thought we could walk home together. Come on, Ken.'

Ken glared at her. 'I need to talk to Cassandra.'

'Ken, don't tell her anything! I read her mind. She's a fake!'

'How dare you?' Cassandra cried out. 'Get out of here now!'

'I'm not leaving without Ken,' Jenna yelled.

Ken turned to the medium. 'I'm sorry about this. I'll get rid of her.' He grabbed Jenna's arm and dragged her out the door.

'Ken, I'm serious,' Jenna hissed once they'd reached the hall. 'I don't know who she really is, or what she's up to, but she's not a medium. This is a fraud.'

'You're just saying that to keep me from helping her find Stevie's father,' Ken accused her. 'You don't want me to tell her what I can do.'

'It's not just that! I'm telling you, Ken, I swear, I saw something in her mind. And she's not telling the truth.'

Ken couldn't remember ever hearing Jenna sound so fervent before.

'Ken, just do me one favour, OK? Don't tell her today. Think about it.'

'I'm not going to change my mind, Jenna.'

'Just wait till the next seance,' she pleaded. 'It's not like anything can happen now. OK? Please?'

'What difference is one day going to make?'

'I don't know! I just feel like − like it will make a difference.'

That sounded pretty lame to Ken, but he'd never heard Jenna sound so frantic. If it really meant that much to her . . .

He went back into the apartment, where Cassandra and Margaret were talking.

'Um, I have to go.'

'I thought you wanted to talk to me privately,' Cassandra said.

'It can wait till tomorrow,' Ken said.

CHAPTER TEN

THE WOMAN WHO HAD been calling herself Cassandra pulled off her veil and cursed as the door closed behind Ken.

'I think we're all right,' she told Amanda. 'I kept my mind completely blank all the time that girl was in the room.'

Amanda reminded herself that she wasn't Amanda. 'Why?'

'She can read minds,' Serena said. 'But I blocked her from getting into mine.'

'You can do that?'

'I learned how when I studied hypnosis,' Serena Hancock informed her. 'You concentrate on a little phrase called a mantra. Some people do this for meditating, to clear the mind. It can work when you're around mindreaders too. When I was student-teacher in her class I was able to hide my thoughts from her.' She started towards the kitchen. 'I'm going to fix myself a Martini. Do you want one?'

Amanda shuddered. 'No, thanks.' She followed Serena into the kitchen. 'You can't really make contact with spirits, can you?'

Serena stared at her. 'Are you being funny? Of course not! You know that.'

Margaret would know that, Amanda thought. 'Oh, sure, but I was just wondering. Maybe, after doing this for a while, you might have developed the gift.'

Serena began mixing her drink. 'It doesn't work like that. You've either got it or you haven't. It's too bad though. If I could connect with dead people, I wouldn't need Ken. I hope he's not going to be a problem. I think he really wants to help Stevie. He seems like the caring type.'

'Yeah, Ken's like that,' Amanda said. Once again Serena looked at her oddly, and Amanda tried to recover. 'I mean, that's how he's been acting here.' Mentally, she scolded herself. She *had* to remember who Serena thought she was. It wasn't easy. She was still reeling from the revelations of the evening before.

'Don't you want anything to drink?' Serena asked.

'Just water,' Amanda said. 'I . . . um . . . I'm on a diet. Excuse me, I'm going to wash my hands.'

It was just an excuse to be alone in the bathroom for a few minutes. She put the lid down on the toilet and sat there.

She had to admit, Serena had designed a very clever scheme. Fortunately, when Amanda had learned who Serena was the night before, the shock had left her speechless and she was able to learn a lot about the plan by just listening to Serena talk about it.

She gathered that Margaret and Serena were friends from back in the days when they'd studied to become teachers at the same university. Teachers didn't make much money, and Serena wanted a lot more than she earned. And it appeared that Serena was still obsessed with getting her hands on a winning lottery ticket.

From what Amanda had figured out, Serena had learned about Stevie's plight from another friend, Jane, who taught at a different school. Stevie was in Jane's class, and he'd confided in his teacher. Jane was so moved and saddened by the story, she'd mentioned it in passing in a conversation with Serena. And Serena – without telling Jane, of course – came up with a plan.

Having done some of her student teaching at Meadowbrook in the gifted class, she'd learned about their special gifts. She knew what Ken could do, and she thought he'd be able to get in touch with Stevie's father. So she set herself up as a medium, contacted Stevie and Ken, and enlisted Margaret to help her out by acting like a satisfied client. This would hopefully convince Ken that 'Cassandra' was a legitimate medium. And as payment, Margaret would get a cut of the money from the lottery ticket.

What Amanda hadn't figured out yet was how Serena would find out the location of the lottery ticket before Ken told Stevie. And she was afraid to ask because she was sure Margaret already knew.

She was also curious about Dahlia's role in all this. But she didn't even have to ask about that. When she returned to the living room, the Martini seemed to have put Serena in a talkative mood.

'This is going even better than I expected,' Serena

mused. 'We really lucked out when Dahlia showed up. That was a good idea you had.'

What idea was that? Amanda wondered. 'You think so?' she asked carefully.

'Obviously – Dahlia would never have turned up if she hadn't read the ad you put about me in the newspaper.' Serena laughed. 'What a crackpot. She really believes she had these other lives. And she's so gullible! She's falling for everything I've told her.'

Amanda got it. Dahlia was giving the whole scam more credibility.

'Ken is totally sympathetic to Stevie,' Serena continued. 'Tomorrow I'm going to tell him I sense that he has a special connection with the spirit world. I'll ask him to help me locate Stevie's father.'

She yawned and set down her empty glass. 'I can't keep my eyes open.'

'I'm tired too,' Amanda said quickly. 'I guess I'd better be going home.'

'By the way,' Serena said, 'you were better tonight. But you need to be a little more emotional about your mother, the way you were last Friday.'

'OK,' Amanda said.

'Oh, and I need you to do me a favour.' Serena went to a desk and took a piece of paper from a drawer. 'Go to the pharmacy tomorrow and get this prescription filled.'

'What is it?' Amanda asked, taking the paper.

Serena rolled her eyes. 'What do you think?' She walked Amanda to the door. 'See you tomorrow. And try to be a little more pathetic, OK?'

On the way to the bus stop, Amanda paused under a street light and tried to read the prescription. The handwriting wasn't easy to read, but she could tell it was one of those medical words that didn't mean anything in regular English. Beziterol or Besiteral – something like that. She had no idea what it was for.

Thank goodness for the Internet. As soon as she was back in Margaret's apartment she sat down at Margaret's laptop and went online. On her third attempt at deciphering the word, she hit the jack-pot.

The search engine had taken her to a dictionary of drugs. She skipped over the chemical words, and came to a definition of Besiterol that she could understand.

'A highly potent and fast-acting insomnia medication. To be used with extreme caution.'

Amanda didn't think Serena had insomnia. She'd been falling asleep tonight after one Martini. And then it clicked – Amanda knew how Serena was going to get the lottery-ticket location before Ken gave the information to Stevie. Somehow she'd get this medicine into Stevie, and he'd fall asleep while Ken talked to his father. And if Ken didn't willingly offer Serena the information, she could always hypnotize him to get it.

Amanda didn't know what amazed her more – Serena's evil mind, or her own brilliance at figuring it all out. And those classmates of hers thought she was worthless! Well, she'd show them what she could do.

Now she was glad she hadn't been able to tell Ken that she'd snatched Margaret's body. They'd all be surprised and impressed with Amanda when she exposed this nasty scheme all by herself.

Chapter Eleven

KEN HAD NO FAITH in what Jenna had
told him about the medium. He wasn't
stupid. He knew exactly what she was
trying to do, and this had nothing to do with anything she claimed to find in Cassandra's mind. Jenna
just didn't want him to reveal his gift, and she'd say
anything to keep him from helping out at the seance.

He'd been furious at her when she stormed into
the seance, but after sleeping on it, and thinking
about it, he wasn't angry any more. He thought he
knew why Jenna had tried to stop him from getting
involved.

She was scared. She believed all that stuff Madame
said about the enemies who were out to get them,
and Ken supposed there could be some truth in it
for some of the people in the gifted class.

But the bad guys weren't out to get *him*.

What bad guys?

Ken frowned. *Jack, I wish you wouldn't just jump into my head like that. I'm entitled to my private thoughts.*

Hey, man, we never had secrets from each other. What bad guys are you thinking about?

Madame says we can't let anyone know about our gifts because there are bad guys out there who want to use us.

What could they use you for?

Not a clue.

Besides, who's going to believe you can talk to dead people?

Lucy believes, Jack pointed out.

Yeah, I bet that's just because she wants *to believe so she can keep in touch with me. I don't think she'll ever get over me.*

Uh, Jack . . .

What?

I'm sure Lucy misses you a lot, but she's getting on with her life. I mean, she wants to go out with other guys.

Not Simon Dowell!

No . . .

Who, then?

Ken sighed. *Me.*

You're kidding!

Honestly, Jack, I tried to play the big brother role, but I guess she misinterpreted it. She thinks I want to go out with her.

Do you?

No! But how am I going to let her down easy?

There was a long silence before Jack responded again.

You could.

I could what?

Go out with her.

Are you crazy?

Really, Ken. I don't want her to go out with jerks, guys who are going to put the moves on her. I trust you. And if the other guys think she's with you, they won't bother you.

Jack! I don't want to go out with Lucy!

Why not? You don't like that Amanda chick any more, right? And there's nothing wrong with Lucy. Don't you think she's hot?

She's OK, she's just not my type. Jack, I don't want to start anything with Lucy.

Aw, c'mon, be a pal. You don't know how rough it is for me, thinking about her, not knowing what she's doing, who she's seeing . . . Can't you do this for me? Please?

It was Ken's turn to plead. *Can we talk about this later, Jack? I've got stuff to think about for school.*

OK, OK. But remember, you're my best pal. Don't let me down.

Jack was gone, and Ken could get back to his own thoughts. What had he been thinking about before Jack interrupted? Right, the bad guys. The ones who were *not* out to get him.

It was like he'd said in class – his gift just didn't have any criminal potential. And despite what Madame had said, he honestly didn't think that talking about his gift would endanger anyone else in the class. He just had to convince Jenna that this was true and assure her she had nothing to worry about.

He was prepared to do that in the gifted class that day. He even hurried to class so he could take her aside and have time to talk to her before Madame arrived. But when he arrived at room 209, he changed his mind – even before he went in.

There was a glass window in the door, and he

could see a few students were already there. Jenna, Emily and Tracey were huddled together, obviously having a private conversation. And Ken had a pretty good feeling he knew what it was about. Jenna was trying to get the girls to gang up on him, to stop him from going to the seance and offering to help the medium. He sighed in exasperation. What did they think they could do? Tie him up and sit on him?

No, it was more likely that they were planning to hound him and nag him till he broke down and gave in. Or threaten never to speak to him again. Or cry? No, not those three.

Like he cared anyway. Like these girls were more important than a kid whose family was about to lose their home. As far as Ken was concerned, Jenna, Emily and Tracey were being selfish – more concerned with their own safety than the suffering of others. And the minute they started bugging him, he was going to tell them that.

He opened the door, looking at them in scorn as they practically jumped out of their seats. The three of them wore almost identical guilty expressions. Ken went to his seat and opened a book. But before he began reading, he gave each one of them a long, hard glare.

It was pretty effective. The girls didn't approach him.

Jenna didn't even bring up the subject in class. Actually, she didn't have a chance – Charles and Martin got into an argument about some stupid thing. Martin felt like Charles was making fun of him, and his gift came out. When he attacked Charles, Charles made a light fixture fall on Martin's head. Even though neither of the boys was seriously hurt, it was utter chaos in the classroom. But at least it kept everyone's attention off Ken.

He was still concerned about Jenna's efforts to stop him, and when he arrived early at the seance that evening, he spoke to Cassandra before the others arrived.

'If that girl comes by here tonight, don't let her in. Actually, if *any* girls come by, don't let them in.'

Since he couldn't see Cassandra's face, he had no idea if she was puzzled by his demand. She didn't act disturbed. In fact, she changed the subject.

'I'm glad you're here early, Ken,' she said. 'There's something I want to talk to you about.' She motioned for him to sit on her sofa, and she sat by his side.

She spoke softly. 'Ken, I hope this won't sound presumptuous. I haven't known you very long, and yet I feel as if I *do* know you. In a unique way.'

Ken stared at her. 'I – I don't know what you mean.'

She continued. 'I believe we may have something in common. Something very deep and profound.'

Ken swallowed hard. He didn't know what to say.

'I believe,' Cassandra said, 'that you may have a special awareness of the spirit world. As you know by now, I am receptive to their messages, and thus I am highly sensitive to others who are receptive. I think you and I may have similar gifts.'

Ken nodded. 'I was going to talk to you about that tonight. Sometimes, dead people contact me.'

The medium nodded. 'I suspected this might be the case. And tonight, Ken, I may need your help.'

'With Stevie?'

She pressed her hand gently on his. 'Oh, I was

right – you *are* perceptive! I so desperately want to help this boy find the lottery ticket. But you see . . .' she lowered her head . . . 'I must confess that while I do have a gift, I am not the strongest medium in the world. And for some reason I'm finding it very difficult to communicate with Mr Fisher, Stevie's father.'

'Do you actually think I can help?' Ken asked. 'I've never even tried to contact spirits. They come to me.'

'If spirits can find you, you can find them,' Cassandra said. 'With my assistance, of course. Will you try? For Stevie's sake?'

Ken nodded. 'Absolutely.' Then he asked, 'Could we keep this just between us? I don't want everyone to know I have a gift. No offence, but I don't want to get into the medium business.'

'Don't worry,' Cassandra said. 'They won't even be aware of what's going on. You just pass whatever you learn on to me.'

Margaret arrived at the apartment then, followed by Stevie and then Dahlia.

'Margaret, could you help me in the kitchen for

a minute?' Cassandra asked. The two women disappeared into the other room.

'How ya doing?' Ken asked Stevie.

Stevie actually smiled. 'That money you paid me . . . my mother was able to buy Cindy some shoes from the thrift store. They're not new, but at least they fit her and they don't hurt. And she found some cream at a pharmacy that's helping Dena's rash.'

'That's great,' Ken exclaimed. 'So things are better, huh?'

Stevie nodded, but his smile faded. 'But the landlord came around again. He's only giving us another week to get the rent money together.'

'Well . . . maybe by then you'll have the money,' Ken said. He didn't tell the boy about his plan to help the medium because he didn't know if it would work, and Stevie had already had enough disappointments in his life.

Margaret and Cassandra returned, and to Ken's surprise, Cassandra was holding a tray with glasses. Margaret carried a pitcher of red stuff.

'This is homemade strawberry punch,' Cassandra

announced. 'I have a good feeling about tonight – that it's going to be special. So I thought we'd have a little pre-seance celebration.'

'Shouldn't we have the celebration after the seance?' Ken asked. 'I mean, if it's successful?'

'One has to establish the ambience for success,' Cassandra declared as she set the tray down. 'Success is more likely to come when the appropriate feelings are in the air.'

Her reference to 'feelings' bothered Ken. He looked at the punch suspiciously. 'Is there alcohol in this?'

Cassandra let out a tinkling laugh. 'Of course not, Ken. I would never serve an alcoholic beverage to young people. I don't even drink alcohol myself – mediums rarely do. We are afraid it could dull our senses and make us less accessible to the spirits.'

He felt foolish for having asked. He should have known Cassandra would be the responsible type.

'Margaret, will you pour?' Cassandra asked.

Margaret picked up the pitcher and turned her

back to the others to face the coffee table. Ken approached her.

'Can I help?' he offered.

'No!' Cassandra answered for her. 'Margaret can do it herself. Aaah!'

Surprised by the strong reaction, Ken turned to Cassandra. But she wasn't protesting his offer of assistance. The scarves that covered her face were coming off. And they weren't just falling – it was as if invisible hands were ripping them from her.

Invisible hands . . . that could only mean one thing. One person. 'Tracey!' Ken yelled in outrage. She must have followed him! But in an instant his fury turned to something else. Something more closely related to utter shock.

The medium's face had been exposed, and he recognized her.

'You!' he cried out.

At that very moment there was pounding on the door. 'Go away!' Serena Hancock shouted.

'Police! Open this door immediately or we'll break it down!'

'Good heavens!' Dahlia exclaimed. 'Isn't this

exciting?' She went to the door and opened it. Two uniformed police officers strode in. Ken gaped, and his mouth dropped even further when, just behind the policemen, Emily and Jenna entered. And then Tracey was there too.

Emily pointed at the student teacher/medium. 'That's her! That's the woman who threatened me two months ago at Meadowbrook!'

'She's crazy!' Serena screamed.

'I recognize her too,' Jenna declared.

'So do I,' Tracey cried out.

'So do I,' Ken echoed in a whisper. He was still in a state of shock. But somehow he managed to blurt out, 'I think there's a scam going on here.'

One of the police officers produced a pair of handcuffs. As he was locking Serena's hands together behind her back, the woman yelled, 'I'm not going down alone for this.' She jerked her head at Margaret. 'She's in on it too! Margaret Robinson!'

'That's not true!' Margaret declared hotly as the other officer began to cuff her. 'I'm not even Margaret!'

But the police weren't giving either of them

the opportunity to protest further. The two women were hustled out the door, leaving behind three stunned seekers of guidance from the spirit world – and three girls with expressions that were just a little bit smug.

CHAPTER TWELVE

AMANDA WASN'T SURE IF she was frightened or furious or some combination of the two. Sitting on a bench, her back pressed against the wall, she tried in vain to calm down. This just wasn't happening.

She was in jail. Amanda Beeson, the queen bee of Meadowbrook Middle School, was behind bars. OK, it wasn't Amanda Beeson's *body* in the holding cell, but it was Amanda Beeson who felt imprisoned.

She wasn't alone. Serena was there too, pacing the floor, muttering to herself. And there were four other women, none of whom looked very nice. They weren't pacing or shaking or acting nervous though. In fact they all looked like they'd been in prison before. One of them was even sleeping!

Serena-Cassandra glared at her. 'Stop crying!' she snapped.

Amanda hadn't even realized there were tears running down Margaret's face. She certainly had every right to cry. She didn't deserve to be here! She'd even tried to stop Serena's evil scheme from succeeding. The prescription Serena had given her . . . Amanda had had it filled at a pharmacy, but only so she could see what the pills looked like. Back at Margaret's place, she'd emptied the pills into the sink and replaced them with similar-looking little white mints that wouldn't do anyone any harm. While Serena would think Margaret was dropping a sleeping pill into the glass meant for Stevie, he would simply receive a glass of punch with a little mint flavouring. He wouldn't fall asleep. Ken would tell him where the lottery ticket was, Amanda would reveal herself and expose the scheme, and she'd be a hero!

But instead she was one of the villains. A common criminal. Was this the kind of person Margaret was? She wondered if Margaret had ever been in jail before. Maybe Amanda should be acting a little more nonchalant about all this. But what did it matter now? She actually wanted the guards to know she *wasn't* Margaret!

Unfortunately, she really didn't know how she was going to convince them of that. Had anyone ever used bodysnatching as an excuse to be released from a prison? She seriously doubted it. No one would believe her.

There was only one way out of this mess. She had to get out of Margaret's body and back into her own, which at that very moment was probably lying in her nice, soft bed being waited on and coddled by her mother.

She took some deep breaths and tried to think rationally. How had she got out of bodies before? Falling, hitting her head – it was usually something like that. When she had been in-visible-Tracey, an accidental kick in the head had sent her back into herself. During the bank robbery, when she was Sarah, a slip on the floor did the trick.

Tentatively, she leaned back and tapped her head against the wall. Nothing happened. Her head didn't even hurt. She forced herself to bang her head a little harder.

One of the other prisoners, a hard-looking woman with bright red hair, stared at her. 'What are you doing?'

'Nothing,' Amanda said quickly.

The woman sniggered. 'It's not going to work, you know.'

'What?'

'Hurting yourself to get out of here. You'd have to spill some serious blood. And even then you'd only end up in the clinic here. You'd still be behind bars.'

Amanda remembered another kind of shock that had worked in the past.

She thought back to when she occupied Ken's body. During that time, she formed a − a relationship with a dead boy named Rick. When Rick had said he wouldn't contact her any more, she'd been really upset. That strong feeling had pushed her out of Ken and back into herself.

But here she was in jail. Wasn't that shocking enough to get her out of Margaret? Apparently not.

She tried banging her head again, but she was beginning to think she would never be able to hurt herself enough to provide an adequate physical shock. The red-haired woman glared at her.

'Hey, stop that. I told you, it won't work.'

Amanda ignored her and kept thumping her head.

'You're annoying me,' the woman growled. 'If you don't stop, I'll *make* you stop.'

The threat in her tone sounded very real. Amanda stopped. What else could she do to cause herself pain?

She tried pinching her arm. She dug her manicured nails in so hard, she actually saw a tiny drop of blood. But it didn't hurt all that much.

Maybe she needed that mean-looking woman to carry out her threat. The thought of being attacked was so scary, for a moment she thought it might get her out of Margaret. But no such luck. She was going to have to get really and truly beaten up.

She started thumping her head again. The redhead turned to her with a look of fury. But at that moment, a guard appeared.

'Hey, Cassidy.'

Cassidy turned out to be the red-haired woman. 'Yeah?'

The guard opened the door. 'Your lawyer's here.' The woman hurried out.

'I want to make a phone call!' Serena demanded. 'I know my rights – I'm entitled to a phone call!'

'Yeah, yeah, I'll be back in a minute,' the guard muttered.

Amanda noticed that Serena's hands were clenched into fists. And it dawned on her that she could probably get Serena mad very easily, just by confessing who she really was.

And Serena would believe her. She'd been in their class, and even though she hadn't paid much attention to Amanda when she was there, she must have learned about all the gifts. If Amanda could get her good and mad right now, Serena might just go over the edge and slug her – or at least slap her. Really, really hard. And as much as Amanda didn't want to experience that, it could work.

'Serena?'

'What?' Serena snapped.

Amanda got off the bench and came closer to

Serena, within slapping distance. 'I've got something to tell you.'

But that was as far as she got. The guard reappeared. 'OK, Hancock, you can come and make your phone call.'

'About time,' Serena muttered. To Margaret-Amanda, she said, 'I'll get us out of here.'

Great, Amanda thought dismally. And then what? She *had* to get out of this body! She knelt down by the wall and started banging her head again, harder this time.

'Hey, you're going to hurt yourself!' another prisoner yelled. 'Guard! Guard!'

The guard reappeared.

'I think you'd better do something about this nutcase,' the prisoner said.

The next thing Amanda knew she was being dragged out of the cell by two guards, one holding each arm. And then she was in another cell, a smaller one, all by herself. One of the guards spoke to the other.

'Keep an eye on her till I can find something to tie her to the bed.'

The other guard pulled up a chair just outside the cell. 'Don't move,' she ordered Amanda.

Amanda didn't move. She couldn't. She was in a total state of shock. And yet the feeling still wasn't strong enough to get her out of this body.

This couldn't be happening . . .

CHAPTER THIRTEEN

KEN WAS DEPRESSED.

So the whole seance thing had been a scam. Cassandra was Serena Hancock, still trying to get her hands on a winning lottery ticket. That woman Margaret – she must have been her accomplice. Ken assumed the whole dead-mother thing was a made-up story so the medium could seem authentic.

Was Dahlia in on it too? Maybe, maybe not. In the confusion with the police, she'd taken off. The person he was really concerned about was Stevie. He had disappeared too, before Ken could talk to him. The poor kid . . . He must have been totally freaked out when he realized it was a scam.

'Or maybe little Stevie was part of the scam,' Jenna said.

'Stop reading my mind,' Ken barked. They had

stopped at the bowling alley, where there was a cafe. Jenna, Tracey and Emily were celebrating their successful mission with ice cream. Ken had a glass of water.

'Sorry,' Jenna said.

He looked at her stonily. 'You should be. Why didn't you tell me what you were planning to do at the seance?'

'*I* wanted to tell you,' Emily reported, 'but Jenna said we couldn't trust you not to warn the others.'

Ken hadn't taken his eyes off Jenna. 'Maybe if you'd just told me the medium was really Serena Hancock . . .'

'I didn't know for sure,' Jenna said. 'Her mind was really hard to penetrate. Not like yours, Ken. You're totally transparent.'

'Jenna!' Tracey exclaimed in disapproval. She turned to Ken. 'Jenna said this was the only way. She said you were so into the seance thing, we had to shock you into seeing the truth.'

Ken grimaced. 'Oh, really? And since when is it Jenna's business to shock me into seeing things?'

'Oh, for crying out loud,' Jenna said airily. 'You

should be thanking me, Ken. You could have been totally suckered into their little con game. You were really falling for it! You know, I saved your—'

He wouldn't let her finish. 'Just shut up, Jenna! And for your information, Stevie was not part of it. He's eleven years old!'

'So what?' Jenna countered. 'I once saw a documentary on TV about criminals under the age of twelve.'

'Well, Stevie isn't one of them. He was an innocent victim.'

'How can you be so sure of that?' Jenna shot back. 'Did you read his mind?'

Ken knew he wasn't a violent person, and he'd definitely never hit a girl. But right now, he was feeling very close to a complete change of character, so he did the only thing he could think of doing. He turned away from the girls and headed to the exit.

'Ken! Ken, wait up!'

He turned to find Lucy coming towards him. Could the evening get any worse?

'Do you like bowling?' she asked. 'I love to bowl!

Maybe we could bowl together sometime soon. Like, what are you doing this weekend?'

'Lucy, could you bug off? Can't you take a hint? I don't want to go out with you!' And he stormed out the door.

Once outside, he started walking, fast. He knew he'd been horribly rude and unkind to Lucy, but he felt propelled by an anger that was out of his control. He wasn't sure if he was more angry at himself or at Jenna – himself for being so gullible, Jenna for sticking her nose in his affairs. And for suggesting poor Stevie was part of the whole nasty business . . .

He slowed down. What she had said to him . . . 'Ken, did you read Stevie's mind?' Was she saying that she *had* read his mind?

But how could Stevie be in cahoots with Serena? He was looking for his father's lottery ticket, and he only went to Serena because he thought she was a real medium who could contact his father.

Unless . . . unless . . . the kid in the seance wasn't really Stevie Fisher. Maybe he'd just heard about the situation, and he was pretending to be the boy whose father had died. Or maybe he was some kind of juvenile actor who Serena had hired to *play* Stevie. And they were both waiting for Ken to make contact with Mr Fisher so they could steal the lottery ticket before the real Stevie found it.

There was only one way Ken could know for sure. He had to find the kid who called himself Stevie Fisher.

He looked at his watch. It was almost nine o'clock and this was a school night, which meant he was expected home at ten and he had no idea where Stevie Fisher lived.

But he had his mobile phone. And his mobile phone had Internet access.

He took it out of his pocket, hit the web button, and got a search engine. But now what? He doubted that Stevie had a phone number listed under his own name, and he didn't know the name of Stevie's mother or his late father. Fisher was a common name – there could be hundreds of them.

And then he had a better idea. He accessed the town newspaper, which had its own search capability. He typed in the name Fisher and added the word which just might give him the Fisher he was seeking: obituary.

Bingo! There it was – an obituary from two months ago. Melvin Fisher, age forty-two, of seventy-two Apple Creek Road. Killed in an automobile accident.

What did people do before mobile phones? Ken wondered. Within seconds he had a map on the little screen and directions to Apple Creek Road.

When he arrived, he found a dead-end street lined with small cottage-style homes. He approached the door of number seventy-two, but he didn't get close enough to knock.

A window opened and a voice called out, 'What are you doing here?'

Ken sighed with relief. The boy he knew as Stevie Fisher was looking through the window.

'I just wanted to see if you were OK,' he said. 'You disappeared when the police arrived.'

'No kidding,' the boy said. 'I didn't want them thinking I was one of you people.'

'What do you mean?' Ken asked, walking towards the window.

'Don't come any closer or I'll call the police myself!' Stevie yelled. 'How come you're not locked up?'

'Because – because –' Ken sputtered, 'I wasn't in on it! I thought it was a real seance too!'

'Yeah, right. Just get out of here.' Stevie slammed down the window.

Ken couldn't believe it. Stevie thought *he* was in league with the fake medium. Now he was even more depressed.

He was late getting home, but fortunately his parents were caught up in watching a soccer game on TV and hadn't noticed the time.

'Join us,' his father called from the den. 'It's a terrific game.'

'No thanks,' Ken said. 'I'm kind of beat. I'm going to bed.'

He knew his parents were probably looking at each other in bewilderment, and his mother was wondering if he was sick. They didn't think anything was more important to Ken than soccer, even if he didn't play himself any more. He loved his parents, but there was so much they didn't know about him.

In his room, he flopped down on the bed and

stared at the ceiling. He certainly hadn't lied to his parents about being tired. He was thoroughly, utterly exhausted by the bizarre chain of events that had made up the last few hours. He hoped he would be able to fall asleep easily. He didn't want to think about this crummy day.

Ken?

Not now, Jack. I'm beat. And I've had a really bad day.

I just wanted to tell you . . . I'm sorry.

About what?

About what I asked you to do for me. About going out with Lucy.

The experiences of the past couple of hours had practically erased Jack's request from his memory. And he flushed as he recalled how awful he'd been to Lucy at the bowling alley.

Jack . . . I really don't want to do that.

It's OK. I shouldn't have asked you.

He sounded . . . different. Not sad, not happy, just sort of . . . calm.

I've been thinking a lot, Jack went on. *And I've been getting some help.*

From who?

I can't really say. You wouldn't understand.

Ken had a sudden image of Jack surrounded by a bevy of kind and wise angels. Jack was right – wherever he was right now, Ken could never understand.

So, it's OK if I don't go after her?

Yeah. You see, I've got to let go.

Of Lucy?

Of everything. I have to let go of my life. And I have to stop asking you to live a life for me. I gotta get into where I am now.

So – you're not going to talk to me any more? With a pang, Ken realized that he would miss hearing from Jack.

Oh, we can still talk. I'm just not going to be asking you to do me any more favours.

Oh. OK.

You said you had a really bad day. What happened?

Long story. Can I tell you tomorrow? I need to get some sleep.

Sure. And if Lucy keeps coming on to you, feel free to blow her off.

I already did, Ken thought dismally. He wondered if he could drum up the energy to sit down at his computer right now and compose an apologetic email to her.

Hello, can you hear me?

He thought Jack had gone.

Yeah, I hear you.

Excuse me, I'm sorry to disturb you . . .

Well, it definitely wasn't Jack. He'd never be so polite.

I need your help. It's important.

Look, I'm sorry, but this isn't a good time, OK? Would you mind going away?

Please, young man, you could save my family!

Right. They were always dramatic, these spirits or ghosts or whatever they were.

Another time, OK?

It won't take long. I just want to tell you where I left a lottery ticket . . .

CHAPTER FOURTEEN

AN HOUR LATER, WHEN the guard finally returned, Amanda did something she'd only done once before in her life, when she wanted her parents to buy her real diamond studs for her pierced ears.

She begged.

'Please, please, please, don't tie me up! I promise I won't hit my head against the wall again! Honestly, I swear to you, I won't!'

The guard didn't even look at her. She spoke to the other guard.

'Let her out. She made bail.'

Amanda jumped up. 'You're kidding! Who bailed me out?'

But these guards apparently never shared any more information than they absolutely had to. The guard opened the door, and Margaret-Amanda made a hasty exit. She was directed down a hall and told to go through the last door on the right.

She was clinging to one big hope — that Jenna had read her mind when she was in Cassandra-Serena's apartment. Jenna was the only person who just might know that the Margaret Robinson who was arrested at the seance was really Amanda Beeson. And Amanda made a promise to herself. If this was the case, and Jenna had arranged to get her out of jail, Amanda would never be mean to Jenna again. She would never criticize her or laugh at her behind her back — or in front of her either. She'd even persuade her own personal friends to let Jenna into their clique.

But she started regretting her promises even before she reached the door. Jenna would never fit into Amanda's clique. She had the wrong style, the wrong personality, the wrong everything.

So it was almost a relief when she walked through the door and found that Jenna wasn't waiting for her. But someone else was.

'Come on,' Serena said, leading the way out of the room and down the hall, towards the main doors.

'I've got a taxi waiting for us outside.'

'Who bailed us out?' Amanda asked.

'Very funny,' Serena snapped. 'Really, Margaret, I'm not in the mood for jokes.'

Amanda was on the verge of telling her that she wasn't Margaret, but she didn't think this was the right time or place. Serena probably wouldn't slap her right in front of a police station, and even if she did there was no guarantee it would send Amanda back into her own body. Besides, the idea of a taxi taking her back to Margaret's apartment was a lot more appealing than walking or looking for a bus stop.

They settled into the back of the taxi, and Serena gave the driver an address that was unfamiliar to Amanda. It was neither Serena's address nor Margaret's.

'Where are we going?'

'Where do you *think*?' Serena retorted. 'Honestly, Margaret, what's the matter with you? Did one hour in a jail cell turn your brain to mush?'

Amanda managed a weak smile. 'I guess I'm just a little tired.'

'Yeah, me too,' Serena said, sinking back in the seat. 'Not to mention extremely aggravated. I really thought we'd score tonight. We were so close! I could taste that lottery ticket!'

'Yeah, me too,' Amanda murmured.

'I can't believe Ken went and told his idiot class-mates about the seance,' Serena went on. 'When I was the student teacher in that class they barely talked to each other – they were like strangers.'

She was right, Amanda realized. A lot had changed since those days when she herself had first entered room 209, just before Serena appeared as a student teacher. Not that she would call any of them her best friends now or even invite them to a party.

But they'd shared some very peculiar stuff, and they'd helped each other in and out of some very weird situations. A strange sort of bond was form-ing. She just had to be very careful that the rest of Meadowbrook Middle School never found out or her reputation would be in tatters.

'Do you think Stevie will ever find the lottery ticket?' she asked Serena.

'Who knows?' Serena shrugged off the question.

'Who cares? It won't be ours.' She sighed. 'Well, it's no big deal. It would have been nice to have the two million, but we've got bigger stuff in the works.'

Amanda choked back the words 'we do?' Apparently, she and Serena were connected well beyond the seance scheme. What kind of terrible activities were next on the agenda?

This wasn't the life for her. Among the many fantasies Amanda had entertained for her future, being a criminal just wasn't one of them. All the money in the world wasn't worth the churning, sickening feeling she had right now in the pit of her stomach.

But if she was stuck in Margaret Robinson's body, what were her options? Serena was dangerous. She wasn't just going to let Margaret walk away from a life of crime. In the back of her mind, she started considering the various possibilities. Those parents in Florida . . . She could go down there and stay there, far away from Serena Hancock. It wouldn't be easy pretending to be Margaret in front of Margaret's own parents though. She'd managed to do it with Tracey's parents, but that hadn't been so difficult since Tracey's parents had never paid much attention to her. From that phone conversation she'd had with Margaret's mother, she got the feeling they were a lot closer. Mrs Robinson might be able to see that a stranger was occupying her daughter's body.

If she could find the code for Margaret's bank account, she could take all her money – but how much money would a substitute teacher have? She could buy a flight with one of Margaret's credit cards and flee the country, but that meant having a passport, which meant providing documents like birth certificates – assuming Margaret didn't have one already. She had no idea how to get her hands on stuff like that, and she hadn't found a passport on any of her hunts through Margaret's apartment. And even if she did make it to, say, France, what would she do there? She couldn't even speak the language.

Suddenly she felt like she was going to throw up. But she was too scared even to do that.

The taxi pulled up at an ordinary medium-sized house on a tree-lined street. Amanda started to breathe a little easier. This didn't look very scary. Serena turned to her.

'Ready?'

For what? Amanda wanted to ask. But she just managed a weak smile and nodded.

'Remember,' Serena said as they went up the path to the front door, 'we're members of the team too. And they've all had missions that didn't work out. The big project is still on schedule. I realize that this is the first time you'll be meeting them, but don't let them intimidate you.'

'I won't,' Amanda whispered.

'And let me do the talking.'

Amanda was perfectly willing to go along with that.

Serena had a key to the front door. They walked into a foyer which led into a bland, ordinary living room.

'Hello?' she called out.

'We're in here.' The voice was masculine and deep. Amanda thought it sounded vaguely familiar.

She followed Serena into another room, where three people sat at a dining table. And none of the three was a stranger to Amanda.

The first one she recognized was Clare. Her hair was blonde again, the way it had been when

Amanda-as-Sarah had been kidnapped by her.

Next to her was the man she knew as Stuart Kelley, who had claimed to be Jenna's father.

And on the other side of Clare sat Mr Jackson, the principal of Meadowbrook Middle School.

None of them looked at her with any particular interest. Why would they? They'd never seen her before — or so they thought.

But Amanda had seen all of them before, in different places, and in circumstances that were completely unconnected. Or so she'd thought. And the realization of what she was now seeing stunned her. She was dizzy, her head was spinning. Reeling actually. She didn't think that she'd ever had a greater shock.

Which could explain why she suddenly found herself lying in her very own bed with a very sore throat.

CHAPTER FIFTEEN

WHEN HE WOKE UP the next morning, still dressed in the clothes he'd worn the day before, Ken's first action was to check to see if an open notebook lay on the nightstand by his bed. With enormous relief, he found it.

So it hadn't been a dream. And he'd done the right thing – he'd written the instructions down. He read them over and over, until he committed them to memory.

It was early – his alarm wasn't set to go off for another two hours. This was good news, as he had a lot to do before the start of school. As he took a shower and changed his clothes, he went over the plan. He would go back to the Fisher house and catch Stevie before he left for school. He'd tell the boy how he'd had a message from his father, and he'd show him where his father had left the lottery ticket. He bet Stevie would be really surprised to know that his father had a secret place where he kept important things – under a loose floorboard in the back of a rarely visited cupboard full of old junk.

Stevie's mother could cash in the lottery ticket and save the family home. Little Dena could see a real doctor about her rash, and Cindy could have a new pair of shoes. And best of all – for Ken at least – Stevie would know that Ken was a good guy, that he had never been a part of Serena's scheme to steal the ticket. Maybe he and Stevie would remain friends and Ken could be like a big brother to him.

There was only one small problem. Two, actually. First of all, Stevie wasn't going to be very happy to see Ken back at the Fisher house. Ken was going to have to do a lot of fast talking to persuade Stevie to let him in.

But it was the second problem that really made him nervous. To accomplish this task, he would have to let Stevie know about his gift.

He'd argued with Madame and others in the class about this. He hadn't believed that his gift had any value to whatever enemies the class had, and he'd been sure that none of the others in the gifted class would be in danger if he revealed his gift.

Well, events of the past week had proved he was wrong about the first part of his assumption. Bad people *had* tried to use him. And if he could be wrong about that, he could be wrong about putting the class in danger.

But Stevie needed that ticket. And now that Ken knew where the ticket was, how could he do nothing? How could he let Stevie and his family suffer – lose their home, live in poverty – when they didn't have to?

His mother was in the kitchen when he came downstairs.

'What are you doing up so early?' she asked him.

At that moment, Ken learned that he wasn't such a bad liar after all. 'I've got a meeting at school with my science project group.'

His mother was impressed. 'Well, you kids must be excited about this project if it's getting you out of bed. What is your group doing?'

He couldn't lie *that* well. He looked at his watch.

'Oh wow, I'm late. I'll tell you about it later, Mom.'

'Don't you want something to eat?' his mother called after him, but he just yelled back another whopper.

'No, thanks, I'm not hungry.' And he was out the door.

But now what? He still hadn't worked out how he was going to fix Stevie's problem.

His mobile rang. He flipped it open and held it to his ear.

'Hello?'

'Ken, this is Tracey. I hope I didn't wake you up.'

He scowled. What did *she* want? He was still very much annoyed by the way the three girls had behaved. 'No, I'm up. What do you want?'

'I couldn't sleep, I felt so bad about yesterday. We shouldn't have made those plans without telling you.'

'It was Jenna's idea, wasn't it?'

'Yeah, but Emily and I went along with it, so we're just as guilty.'

Ken doubted that. He knew how pushy Jenna could be. And Tracey sounded really sorry.

'It's OK,' he relented.

'I wish I could make it up to you,' Tracey said, sounding sincere.

Ken stood very still. A brilliant idea had struck him.

'Actually, Tracey, you can. If you're really sorry, you can help me do something right now.'

He told her all about his visit to Stevie's house the night before, and explained that he now knew where the ticket was. Then he told her his new idea. Ten minutes later, they met up at a corner halfway between their two homes.

Tracey was nervous. 'It doesn't always work, you know. I mean, I'm getting better, but sometimes I just can't do it. And even when it *does* work, I never know how long it will last.'

But she completely understood why he'd come up with his plan. And she was willing to try as hard as she could to make it happen.

When they arrived at Apple Creek Road, Ken pointed out the house.

'I can't walk through walls, you know,' Tracey reminded him. 'I'm going to have to wait for some-one to come in or out.'

Ken looked at his watch. 'Stevie should be leaving for school pretty soon. Can you get ready now?'

He told her about the cupboard and the loose floorboard. Tracey nodded.

'OK. Here goes,' she said. She stood very still and closed her eyes.

'What does it feel like?' Ken asked curiously.

She opened her eyes. 'Be quiet. I have to concentrate.'

'Sorry,' Ken said.

He'd never seen the process in action before. Tracey had developed her gift back when her parents ignored her and she felt invisible. She was a much happier person now, and Ken knew it had to be difficult for her to recapture the feeling of being a nothing, a nobody.

But she did it. Right there, before his eyes, she began to fade. It was positively eerie, like watching a special effect in a science fiction movie. And then she wasn't there.

'Tracey?' he asked.

She must have already taken off. He looked at the

house across the street. He couldn't see her, of course, but if she was following the plan she was waiting just by the door.

Something could still go wrong, and Ken knew it. Maybe Stevie had already left for school, or maybe he wasn't going to school today. Maybe nobody would go in or out of the house at seventy-two Apple Creek Road all day. Maybe, maybe, maybe . . .

But he could stop tormenting himself. The door of the house opened. Ken ducked behind a tree and peered through the branches. A woman stood there – Stevie's mother, Ken guessed. She had a small child in her arms. That had to be Dena.

An older girl appeared at the door, and then Stevie was there too. They kissed their mother. Then they started walking away, the mother went back inside, and the door closed.

Ken let out the breath he'd been holding. There had been plenty of time for the invisible Tracey to get inside. Now she had to stay invisible long enough to accomplish her mission, and get herself back outside.

Ken stared at the house, even though there wasn't

really anything to look at. It was weird, not having a clue as to what was going on inside.

An eternity seemed to pass. He kept looking at his watch, and he could see that only a few minutes had gone by, but it felt like much longer.

The door to the house opened again, and Mrs Fisher came out. She was holding little Dena's hand. With the other, she locked the front door. Oh no! Ken thought. Would Tracey be trapped inside until someone came home?

'I'm here.'

He looked in the direction of the voice. 'Tracey?'

Even though he couldn't see her face, he could hear the excitement in her voice.

'I found it, Ken! It was right where you said it would be, under the loose floorboard in the cupboard.'

'What did you do with it?'

'I put it on the refrigerator door, under a magnet. They can't miss it.'

Ken frowned. 'Isn't that a little obvious? I mean, wouldn't they have noticed it before?'

'Haven't you ever searched everywhere for something and then found it, right in plain sight?'

She had a point.

'I guess we better get back to school. We've got a long way to go.'

'Yeah, OK.'

'And you can come back now,' Ken added. 'Nobody's watching.'

'Actually . . . I can't.'

'What do you mean?'

'Well, it's weird. I'm getting better and better at disappearing when I want to, but it's not so easy to make myself reappear. It's like, the invisibility has to wear off on its own.'

'How long does that take?'

'I never know exactly. But it's usually within an hour or so. I should be OK by the time we get to school.'

Ken found it surprisingly easy to talk to an invisible Tracey as they walked back to Meadowbrook. He considered holding his mobile to his ear, so anyone passing by wouldn't think he was talking to himself, but he was too happy to really care.

'So, things are going to be all right for Stevie and his family,' he said.

'Yeah. Of course Stevie won't ever know that you found the ticket for him. He'll still think you're one of the bad guys who tried to steal it.'

'I know. I'll just have to live with that.' He was disappointed, but he knew it was for the best, because this way he didn't have to tell Stevie about his gift. 'Speaking of bad guys . . . do you get freaked out when Madame keeps talking about how much danger we're in?'

'Not so much,' Tracey replied. 'Not for myself, at least. If I can disappear, no one can really hurt me. I worry about everyone else though.'

'Including me?'

'Sure. You didn't think bad guys would be interested in your gift, and look what just happened.'

'So I suppose we really should try to keep our gifts secret.'

'Absolutely,' Tracey declared. And then she laughed.

'What's so funny?'

'I'm thinking about kids at school – regular

people, not criminal types. If they found out what each of us can do . . .'

'How do you think they'd react?' Ken asked.

'Well, unless they see us in action,' Tracey said, 'we've got nothing to worry about.'

'What do you mean?'

'Think about it, Ken. Hi, guys, guess what I can do? I can disappear! You know Jenna Kelley? She can read minds. Emily sees into the future, and Ken talks to dead people.'

'I think I get your point,' Ken said. 'They wouldn't believe it.' He remembered Jack telling him the same thing.

'Exactly. I mean, I wouldn't go around talking about what we can do. But if a rumour starts spreading around school, well, I don't think we have anything to worry about. By the way, do you know where Amanda went? The real Amanda?'

'No. Maybe she'll be back at school today and we'll find out.'

'I think it could be fun to live someone else's life for a while,' Tracey said. 'If you could be anyone else for a week, who would you be?'

They were able to entertain each other with candidates all the way back to Meadowbrook. Tracey wanted to go into space as an astronaut or be a jockey on a horse that could win the Kentucky Derby. Ken admitted to a secret dream of performing as a hip-hop artist. They were so caught up in their fantasies that Ken completely forgot he was talking to someone who wasn't physically there. He only remembered as the school came into view.

'Better lower your voice,' he cautioned Tracey as they approached the building. 'Actually, it's still early, there aren't many people around. But we probably ought to stop talking before anyone notices us.'

'They can't hear me,' Tracey told him. 'You're the only person who's ever been able to hear me when I'm invisible.'

'I guess I'm just more sensitive to people who aren't really there,' Ken replied.

'I can't believe I'm still invisible,' Tracey grumbled. 'I hope I'm back by this afternoon – I've got an appointment for a haircut.'

Ken didn't reply. He'd just spotted Lucy standing alongside the stairs leading up to the main entrance. She was alone, and when she spotted him, she waved.

He winced. He hadn't written that apologetic email yet. He was going to have to apologize in person. Well, so be it. He squared his shoulders and started towards her. It dawned on him that Tracey might still be by his side, and he should tell her to go on, that this was something personal. But now it was too late. Lucy would be able to see him speaking to no one if he did talk to Tracey.

He tried to put his companion out of his mind and focus on the girl in front of him. 'Hi, Lucy. Listen, I want to apologize for last night. I was in a really bad mood about something, and I took it out on you. I'm really sorry.'

She didn't seem upset. 'That's OK, I forgive you,' she said with a smile. 'As long as you take me to the eighth-grade dance this weekend.'

'I'm in the ninth grade, Lucy.'

'I know that! But we're allowed to bring people from other grades as our dates.'

He took a deep breath. 'Listen, Lucy . . . you're a

cute girl and all, but – well – I'm sort of into someone else.'

He could have sworn he heard a sharp intake of
breath, like a gasp, and it hadn't come from Lucy.
Damn! Tracey was still there. And now she'd want
to know who Ken was talking about.

Lucy didn't seem to care. 'Well, she's out of luck,
whoever she is. Because I want you to be into me.'

Ken shifted his weight from one leg to the other.
This was not going to be easy. 'Like I said, Lucy . . .
you're really nice, and I know Jack was crazy about
you, but I'm just not interested in you that way. I
hope we can be friends, but . . .' His voice trailed off
as her expression changed. There was something cold
in her face now.

'Don't forget, Ken, I know something about you.'

He looked at her stupidly. 'Huh?'

'I know what you can do. How would you feel
if I told people that you talk to dead people?'

It was Ken's turn to gasp. 'Lucy! You wouldn't do
that, would you?'

'Not if you go to the dance with me. And other
places.'

It took Ken a moment to respond. 'Are you – are you trying to blackmail me?'

Lucy laughed, but it wasn't a pretty laugh. There was something very mean about it. 'I never thought I'd have to threaten a guy to go out with me, but I'll do what I have to do. I want you to be my boyfriend, Ken. I think we'd be good together, and once you get over your hang-ups about me being Jack's ex-girlfriend, you'll be happy with me.'

'Lucy, this has nothing to do with Jack. No offence, but I'm just not into you!'

Her voice hardened. 'Then *get* into me. Or everyone at school is going to know about your weird conversations.'

He couldn't believe what he was hearing. 'You'd really do that?'

'Sure.'

He looked at her thoughtfully.

'Well?' she asked, smiling.

He smiled back. 'Go right ahead.'

Her smile faded. 'What?'

'Tell them. Tell everyone I hear dead people. Write

an article for the school newspaper. Or announce it over the intercom.'

She was speechless. Ken's smile broadened.

'Because it's not like anyone's going to believe you,' he said. 'I gotta go. Hope you find someone to take you to the dance.'

He knew Tracey was by his side as he walked into the school. She was still invisible, but he could have sworn there was a huge grin on her invisible face.

Chapter Sixteen

EVEN WITH HER SORE throat, Amanda had never before been so incredibly happy to be back in her own body. She felt so good, she insisted on going back to school. And for the first time ever, she was impatient to get through the day so she could go to the gifted class.

She had so much to tell them! Even Madame would be impressed with her adventure. Of course Jenna would claim to be the hero, since she had organized the revelation of the medium's true identity. But Amanda could top that. She had the most amazing, stupendous news of all. There was a conspiracy, just as Madame had suggested. People who'd tried to use the gifted students were working together. And their very own school principal was part of the gang.

Just before class, she went into a bathroom to touch

up her lipgloss and brush her hair. She wanted to make a grand entrance, so she stayed there until the warning bell rang, and then dashed down the hall.

She entered just as the final bell rang. From her desk, Madame looked up and smiled.

'Welcome back, Amanda! How are you feeling?'

'A little tired,' Amanda said, 'but not from the operation.' She addressed the whole class. 'You'll be surprised to learn I haven't been spending the last few days in bed.'

Jenna spoke. 'We're not surprised. Tracey told us.'

Amanda stared at her. 'Tracey told you *what*?'

'Emily and I went to visit you at the hospital,' Tracey said. 'We knew it wasn't you.'

Amanda hadn't realized Tracey was there. Neither had Madame.

'Tracey! Where did you come from?'

The newly visible Tracey explained. 'Ken wanted to help his friend from the seance, Stevie, to find his father's lottery ticket.'

Ken picked up the story. 'His father spoke to me last night and told me where the ticket was. I wanted to tell Stevie myself but I came up with a better plan that meant I didn't have to reveal my gift. I asked Tracey if she could turn herself invisible, get the ticket, and put it somewhere the family was bound to see it.'

Madame looked pleased. 'Very good, Ken. You managed to keep the secret *and* help Stevie's family. Well done!'

Now everyone was congratulating Ken and Tracey. Amanda was starting to feel as if *she* was invisible.

'Isn't anyone interested in knowing where I went when I left my body?' she asked loudly.

'Let me guess,' Charles said. 'Someone who wasn't getting their tonsils taken out.'

'No kidding,' Jenna remarked. 'You know, Amanda, I never thought you had a very useful gift – at least not for helping anyone else – but it certainly works for *you*. You can get out of doing anything you don't want to do.'

Amanda was furious. 'For your information, Miss Know-it-all, I happened to be at Ken's seance!'

Ken was clearly startled. 'You're kidding! Who were you?'

Gratified by the attention, Amanda preened. 'Margaret Robinson, the woman who claimed her mother had just died. But who turned out to be Serena's pal!'

'Serena?' Madame asked.

Ken broke in. 'Serena Hancock, that girl who did student-teaching here. She was the fake medium.'

'Good grief!' Madame remarked. 'She's certainly determined to get her hands on a lottery ticket.'

Amanda was about to announce that there was much more to it than that when Madame turned back to her.

'Amanda, if you took over the body of someone involved in this business, you must have realized straight away that it was a scam.'

Amanda nodded proudly. 'I did, and—'

But Madame wasn't finished. She spoke sternly. 'Then you should have come directly here and told me! You put yourself in grave danger, not to mention Ken.'

'And us,' Jenna piped up. 'Me and Emily and Tracey.'

'Why did you do that, Amanda?' Madame wanted

to know. 'Why didn't you tell us what was going on?'

Jenna jumped in again. 'Because she was probably having too much fun being an adult. What did you do, Amanda? Shop till you dropped?'

That got a laugh from several classmates.

'Now, Jenna,' Madame reprimanded her, 'let's hear Amanda's side of the story.'

But Amanda was no longer interested in telling them what she'd learned. They were making fun of her, criticizing her, treating her like a villain! And the way Ken was looking at her now, like she was scum! She was hurt, and she was furious. These people – they didn't deserve to know what she knew.

She made a decision. She was *not* going to tell them about the conspiracy, about Mr Jackson – about anything. She'd keep it to herself. And they'd all be sorry for having picked on her like this.

Because with the information she had, she'd be the one who would save them all from whatever those bad people were planning. She'd be the biggest hero of all. She'd be worshipped and adored and respected. Which was what she deserved.

But for now . . .

'My throat hurts,' she announced. 'Can I go to the infirmary and ask the nurse to call my mother? I think I should go home.'

Madame was immediately sympathetic. 'Of course, Amanda. We can discuss this at another time, when you're feeling better.'

And with her head high and her secret intact, Amanda left the room.

Epilogue

FROM THE FOLLOWING DAY'S newspaper:

FISHER FAMILY FLABBERGASTED!
The family of Melvin Fisher, who died suddenly in an accident two months ago, were finally able to claim the fortune left to them by the late Mr Fisher. Days before the accident that killed him Mr Fisher had purchased a ticket for the weekly lottery, which at that time was worth over two million dollars. While there was evidence that the winning ticket had been sold, no one came forward to claim the prize. Yesterday Mr Fisher's widow Louise Fisher found the lottery ticket under a magnet on her refrigerator door.

Congratulations to Mrs Fisher and her children Stevie, Cindy and Dena, who have been confirmed by the lottery commission as the winners of two million dollars!

A selected list of titles available from Macmillan Children's Books

The prices shown below are correct at the time of going to press. However, Macmillan Publishers reserves the right to show new retail prices on covers, which may differ from those previously advertised.

Marilyn Kaye

Gifted: Out of Sight, Out of Mind	978-0-330-51036-3	£5.99
Gifted: Better Late than Never	978-0-330-51035-6	£5.99
Gifted: Here Today, Gone Tomorrow	978-0-330-51006-6	£5.99

Meg Cabot

Jinx	978-0-330-44201-5	£5.99
The Mediator: Love You to Death	978-0-330-43737-0	£5.99
The Mediator: High Stakes	978-0-330-43738-7	£5.99
The Mediator: Mean Spirits	978-0-330-43739-4	£5.99
The Mediator: Young Blood	978-0-330-43740-0	£5.99

All Pan Macmillan titles can be ordered from our website, www.panmacmillan.com, or from your local bookshop and are also available by post from:

Bookpost, PO Box 29, Douglas, Isle of Man IM99 1BQ

Credit cards accepted. For details:
Telephone: 01624 677237
Fax: 01624 670923
Email: bookshop@enterprise.net
www.bookpost.co.uk

Free postage and packing in the United Kingdom